‘THE BU

Sylvie Short - Author profile

After many years in the teaching profession, Sylvie Short has retired to concentrate on writing full time. As well as ‘The Bubble’ she has written two other books and had three short stories published in a Cambridgeshire magazine. She lives in East Anglia with her husband, Dave.

Many thanks for your encouraging words.
Best wishes,
Sylvie

'THE BUBBLE'

Published in 2010 by New Generation Publishing

First Edition

‘THE BUBBLE’

For

My son, Alex, with thanks for his encouragement and help with proof- reading;

My daughter-in-law, Helen, grandsons, Eden and Francis and, above all, my husband, Dave, without whose endless support and practical help this book would not have reached the publisher.

Acknowledgement

I am also indebted to Keith Harrison for sparing time to share with me his knowledge of both arable and pig farming.

And to Paul Haresnape for assistance in formatting the covers.

‘THE BUBBLE’

'THE BUBBLE'

Chapter 1

Marcus walked quickly into the meeting room; his feet, of course made no sound. The murmur of voices died to a respectful silence as all eyes turned towards him; they knew what they had to say and waited quietly for their turn. He began with Jonas, just looking at him; no question was needed, and the old man cleared his throat,

"Not good news I'm afraid. Murders…rapes…rapes with murders…all up quite considerably on previous figures."

He leafed through the large bundle of papers in front of him, each crisp, white sheet floating over onto the one before the moment his finger touched it. He shook his head in despair,

"What about the judicial system? Surely these crimes are being dealt with more severely now, as we decided."

Marcus waited for a positive response to his question, but was disappointed.

"No, far from it. The prisons are full to bursting, the police understaffed and overstretched, and as for the judges, well…not above corruption themselves I'm afraid."

He leafed again through the papers,

"One here often too drunk to think straight…and this one," he stopped flicking the pages and his finger rested in the centre of one of them,

"Accepted a bribe and let the rapist off with a spell of community service."

The old man sat back still shaking his head and Marcus' piercing eyes moved to the younger man sitting next to him.

"Anthony?"

"Many more cases of men fathering children with their own daughters…I know, I know,"

He held up his hand as he saw Marcus' expression of surprise and disbelief, then continued,

"It's horrendous, disgusting, abhorrent, but it hasn't stopped. Of course we all thought that the case eleven years ago would make people more aware, but they are just as blind…or scared of coming forward as they ever were. And as for the increase in the number of paedophiles, well, let's not go there."

Anthony thumbed through his small mountain of white paper,

"Hundreds…hundreds…and they don't even think they are doing anything wrong."

The meeting continued and each man, armed with his own sheaf of white papers, had a tale of horror to tell. Drunkenness and brawling in the streets worse than before in spite of some efforts to get it under control; burglaries still on the increase, babies tortured by the very people who are supposed to care for them, the government lying and still trying to get out of financial trouble by borrowing even more money they can't afford to repay.

With only three men left who hadn't spoken, Marcus held up his hand. There was silence as he rubbed his eyes,

"There must be some good news."

The assembled company looked at each other but no-one spoke. Marcus tried again,

"What about The Big Man's buildings? Do people still go there?"

There was a ripple of laughter in the room which died very quickly as their leader looked around.

"Sorry, Marcus, that was my fault." The man speaking was Michael, one of the three yet to deliver his report. He continued,

"Before you came in I was telling everyone about the state of The Big Man's buildings. Yes a few still go there, but the message is dying; the leaders continue to dress up in their robes and go through the old sheets that have been around for years but…well, they're all tired, very tired. They spend a lot of time on their knees in The Big Man's buildings which are, I'm afraid, otherwise completely empty."

"And that was amusing was it?" Marcus wasn't amused.

"No…no. What made them laugh was a story I told about last Christmas. There are usually, at this time, vague stirrings in the memories and some do make their way to The Big Man's building, but they are very confused. I saw a crib with no baby, two shepherds and a jolly Father Christmas sitting beaming in the straw."

Marcus didn't laugh.

"Have you anything else to report, Michael? Your brief was, I believe if I remember rightly, to evaluate the growing influence of Celebrity Culture."

The handsome young man looked serious and turned to his sheaf of papers,

"I have done as I was asked and the news is not good. I could elaborate if there were time, but to sum up: With the decline of interest in The Big Man, the glory all goes now to anyone who does anything outrageous and gets themselves noticed. The more outrageous the act, the more they are celebrated. There are no limits."

No-one was smiling now as Marcus turned his attention to the penultimate man in the semi-circle in front of him.

"Joseph?"

"Yes, Marcus, my brief was Community and Environment. Well, in a nutshell, everyone is rushing here, there and everywhere looking for thrills and excitement anywhere except on their own doorstep. No-one has any time for their neighbours, in fact they haven't a clue who their neighbours are and care even less; and the planet is becoming a tip."

"But what about the Green Issues? They were big a few years ago and you reported that things were going well. It was at the time when it suddenly dawned on them that they couldn't keep borrowing money…do you remember? They started looking after the planet, looking for simpler pleasures…"

"I know, but it didn't last. The government borrowed more, told them everything would be alright and encouraged them to go on spending. Now greed is more prevalent than ever. They've forgotten what they were supposed to learn."

Marcus raised an eyebrow in the direction of Joshua, the last man in the line reporting on the state of family life.

"Broken, I'm afraid, Marcus, and this issue is, I believe, directly linked with the Celebrity Culture," he glanced at Michael who nodded in agreement, then continued,

"Everyone sees the so-called celebrities doing exactly what they please with regard to having children with different fathers, not bothering about marriage, that sort of thing and they follow like sheep. Both groups are unhappy, but the difference is that the celebs can afford to fund these shenanigans; the ordinary folk can't, so they end up living on the state. There are just no guidelines."

Marcus sat back,

"There are guidelines. What about the stuff The Big Man sent down? I know it was a long time ago, but nevertheless..."

He paused and, glancing around, saw that a few of the company were trying to suppress smiles. He looked directly at Michael,

"Another story, no doubt." He waited.

"Yes, Marcus. A few years ago they used television and spent hours asking people if they thought The Big Man's guidelines were still relevant in the sophisticated world of today. Of course just about everyone said they weren't, so then they were asked for a modern law that they could all live by. There was much apparent thought and after a great deal of discussion a vote was taken; what they came up with was, 'treat everyone as you would like to be treated.' They were all so busy smirking at their own cleverness and applauding each other, that they completely overlooked the fact that if they did that they would be using at least seven of The Big Man's guidelines. But it made no difference. They still go on killing each other, lying and stealing..."

Marcus stood up. He looked slowly round the assembled Company then spoke very quietly,

"The Big Man suspected that this would be the case; he sent you all down to check, but in his heart he knew what you would say. He goes on loving them in spite of everything, as we've all come to expect, and he wants to give them another chance," He sighed and looked away for a moment, "so many chances..."

"Yes…too many if you ask me."

It was Anthony who spoke and Marcus looked at him; his eyes flashed a warning,

"We didn't ask you, Anthony." He paused and Anthony looked down at his feet, a slow flush creeping up his neck and over his cheeks. Marcus again addressed everyone,

"Maybe now is a good time to remind you all that His compassion, among other things, is what makes Him 'The Big Man;' we do not question but simply obey."

"Sorry, Marcus," Anthony looked again towards the man standing before them, his white tunic ruffled by the gentle breeze which kept the room at a perfect temperature. He raised his right arm high in the air and drew it slowly down towards him, and as he did so a picture appeared, fluid at first as if drawn on water, then gradually becoming still, the ripples disappearing to leave a clear image, an island surrounded by water.

"Oh, the island again," Jonas smiled, "he's always had a weakness for that island."

"Yes, as you say, the island."

Marcus folded his arms and took a few steps forward,

"He has a plan. He wants to use The Bubble."

There were gasps of astonishment and everyone talked at once,

"Impossible…it'll never work…it never has yet…what a risk…"

Marcus held up his hand and there was silence. He knew the Company would have questions and he was happy to answer them. Joseph was the first,

"What about timing?"

Marcus reminded him that time had never been a problem for The Big Man then dealt with rest of the issues, one by one. So absorbed were they all in their discussion that they were unaware of the approach of another person, a young man, who stood and waited quietly at the entrance. Finally Joshua asked the last question, the one they had all wanted to ask, but hadn't dared. He took a deep breath,

"So…who is it, Marcus? Who's going down?" He paused, "Who's been chosen?"

They all sat very still and waited. The task was huge and they each knew that if they were chosen they couldn't refuse. They looked at each other. Jonas was old, no-one knew exactly how old, but maybe if the big man wanted experience and stability….Michael, only twenty five and inclined to be frivolous; still…a sense of humour may be an asset…Anthony, thirty five, dark and handsome…no, too severe and given to occasional outbursts, a bit hot-headed…Joseph, thirty…probably too shy and Joshua, forty…well sensitive, yes, but maybe too sensitive. Age of course wasn't really a consideration; they all stayed the same age as when they were called up, except the babies in the crèche who were called back down again almost immediately as they got another chance. Staying young was seen as one of the compensations of being called up early.

Marcus beckoned and the young man at the entrance walked forward, smiling first at Marcus, then making a small bow to the assembled Company who gaped in astonishment. Marcus put his arm gently around the young man's shoulders and smiled,

"Jack has been chosen." He paused, then continued, "And yes, I know what you are all thinking. Jack, at eighteen, is too young; he is one of the 'new wave,' not yet properly trained, will not know what to do or say and will therefore be in grave danger as was…well, you all know what happened before. But Jack is The Big Man's choice and, as before He will guide him, show him what to do and give him the words to say. Any more questions?

The assembled Company were stunned. Marcus had correctly interpreted their thoughts and answered their unspoken queries. There was nothing more to say. But as they looked at the young man standing in the middle of the room they each knew in their hearts exactly why he had been chosen and that he was the right choice, the only one to go if there was any chance of the Bubble succeeding. It was Jonas who found his voice first and he looked directly at Jack,

"How do you feel about going? Are you prepared? Are you happy?"

Jack smiled,

"Of course."

His voice was clear and full of warmth; in fact the whole room, bright and pleasant before he had entered it, was now suffused with a pale golden glow. Jack was dressed in the same simple, white tunic as the members of the Company, but there was, emanating from him, an indefinable shining quality that radiated around the room, filling every corner. A feeling of peace descended as Jack sat next to Marcus and listened to the detailed explanation of the plan.

By the end of the meeting they were all convinced that the plan had every chance of succeeding, but for one thing and again it was Joshua who plucked up the courage to voice the fear that was upper most in everyone's mind.

"What about The Other One?"

Marcus looked grave and for a moment darkness descended on the Company, almost eclipsing the brightness around Jack.

"The Other One, as we all know, is always a problem. The only answer is to keep silent. The Big Man is more than a match for him, but who knows to what depths he will sink. The Big Man won before, but The Other One was never completely overcome. He could, in some way, cause the unravelling. So silence it is, my friends,"

They left the room, each touching Jack and giving him their own individual messages of hope and goodwill.

'THE BUBBLE'

Chapter Two

2020

Years ago it was that the three villages of Upper West Side, Middle West Side and Lower West Side huddled together for warmth like three old crones before a fire.

A warm wind swept across the land in summer, picking up dust and bending the few sparse trees down to meet soil as black as soot. Clouds scudded across huge skies and old grey buildings squatted like toads on fields – golden, green, black, green again – criss-crossed by dykes and drains.

Winters were hard as iron with white mist rising from the river and snaking down the lanes. Lamps would glow, throwing out fingers of light across the street where, hands in pockets and backs bent, huddled against the cold, people hurried home to their fires and thoughts of Christmas – the Crib Service and bells on Christmas Day.

The greyness would lift and turn to spring, then suddenly summer again with barges drifting lazily along the river and grasses bending towards murky water, silvered by slices of sky. Flowers decorated the Church where people sang in celebration. Butchers in white aprons plied their trade with doors wide open and people fanning themselves against the heat; there were other shops too, everything you needed in plentiful supply. There were barbecues on the river bank with music and laughter, and a harvest celebration to end the summer with huge hams, pies and crumbles made with apples gathered from over laden boughs. Tractors bounced along the lanes bulging with loads of orangey carrots and brown-paper skinned onions; while giant spools of yellow straw, silent sentinels on fields of stubble, sat waiting.

But everything changes, slowly, almost imperceptibly, inevitably everything changes; time captures us in its forward march and on we go; it happens slowly…slowly. We scarcely notice the few brush strokes until the whole picture seems suddenly to have been transformed. That's how it is. That's how it was for the three villages – Upwest, Midwest and Downwest – until Monday 10th January 2020, the day everything, without warning, suddenly changed....

"Mum, put your foot down for Pete's sake, we're going to miss the train and I've got dance first period. We're rehearsing for the show and if I don't get there Melanie Fisher will stand in for me."

Rebekka Thompson who had been leaning forward and pleading with her mother in a voice pitched at irritating whine, threw herself back into her seat and stared moodily out of the window, muttering almost inaudibly,

"...and wouldn't she love that. Cow! She'd whip the part off me if she could...Mum...please!"

Her voice went up again and she spread her hands in a dramatic gesture of total despair.

"Mum....please..."

Her brother Jake, sitting next to her, mimicked the whine and gesture then hissed,

"Shut up, Bekks, for crying out loud, you're giving me earache."

James, their older brother, sat in the front seat next to their mother, oblivious to everything around him as his body moved rhythmically in time with the music being played into his ear by the tiny machine attached to it.

Carolyn's hands tightened on the steering wheel and she could feel her jaw clench. She spoke slowly.

"Rebekka, it has obviously escaped your notice that I am stuck behind the large lorry in front of me. I cannot overtake as the road is too narrow with bends that prevent me from seeing what is coming. There is a whole queue of traffic and yes we are late. Why are we late? Because you insisted on changing your clothes three times and phoning Kylie twice to talk about things you could have just as easily discussed later in the day at school. Now please do as Jake has suggested and shut up! I'm doing my best."

The gears scraped as she changed down, forced now to go even more slowly by the traffic in front. Furious, Rebekka thrust her fist against her mouth and stared out of the window trying not see Jake grinning, and irritated beyond measure by James' head bobbing about in front of her.

The car wound its way slowly along the village street flanked on either side by a jumble of houses, new builds side by side with old; terraced, detached, semi-detached, thrown together in an apparently arbitrary fashion that made Carolyn wince and sigh every time she passed. There were some beautiful old buildings, examples of quite stunning architecture, all spoilt by the red brick monstrosities squeezed in beside them. Was any thought given to planning? She wondered, or was the local council as powerless now as it had always been? Did any one care? If only she had the time…

Finally at the end of the long street there was a small gap, then one more house before they would be surrounded by fields. Carolyn glanced in the mirror and saw Jake pulling a face; she knew why without even looking out of the window,

"Jake, stop it. You're too old for that nonsense now."

She looked to the right and sure enough there was Martha, the old lady who lived alone in that remote house, chasing her chickens back into their coop. She wobbled from side to side on legs bowed by years of hard work, and wisps of grey hair stuck out from underneath an old felt hat. 'Mad Martha' all the children in the village called her, but at sixteen Carolyn thought Jake should be old enough to tolerate, not mock, eccentricity. Martha did no-one any harm. She kept herself very much to herself but could often be seen collecting stuff from the hedgerows and even pulling up clumps of nettles.

Trying to ignore the frequent snorts of impatience emanating from her daughter, Carolyn looked out to where the fields, crisp with frost, were shining white in the January sunshine; brown earth sprinkled with a dusting of sugar and trees stark and bare against the bright blue sky. She slowed as she approached the cross roads and became aware of stifled giggles from the back seat. Oh, so predictable! Brother and sister, now united, were craning to see in the windows of the shop they were passing, the only shop for miles around, the 'Sex Shop' that the Council had been too weak to prevent from opening there three years ago. At one time the windows would not have been allowed to display their wares so blatantly, 'but now it seems anything goes,' she thought crossly, then felt a little cheered by the fact that she could, at last, pass the lorry and accelerate, minimising the opportunity for prolonged gazing at the contents of the window and therefore reducing the length of time subsequently spent in furtive whisperings. Why, oh why did they have to grow up so quickly!

Carolyn put her foot down and, making good progress along the country road now, thought about the time when they had first moved to Middle West Side seventeen years ago. She was expecting James and she and John had wanted him and any future siblings to be brought up in the country. They had had such plans, so many dreams. The old house was just what they had wanted; she remembered standing hand in hand with John and gazing at the ancient barns at the end of the yard, dreaming of the time when he could give up his job with the insurance company and keep pigs. They would have a small holding, try their hand at self-sufficiency. And maybe she could have a little studio where she would be able to paint and write, there was plenty of room. They had still held onto their dreams even when Jake had come along two years later and Rebekka seventeen months after him. Then Carolyn had gone back to teaching, John had stayed with the same company in Warton, their nearest large town about twenty miles away, and somewhere along the way the dreams had got lost. The time had never seemed quite right somehow, so John was still commuting and she was now head of Bartrum Village School. One thing had led to another; the so called 'credit crunch' of about ten years ago meant that anyone who had a job hung onto it; if you were offered promotion it would have been insane to turn it down in the prevailing economic climate, and of course there were the children and their demands. The modern world dictated that they needed things; their friends had things and they wanted them too.

All was quiet in the car now and, as they approached Bartrum station, Carolyn looked at each one of her children. She loved them dearly, of course, but the teenage years were proving to be as difficult as everyone said they would. She and John had been responsible parents, they had done their best; maybe dreams were best left as just that…only dreams. And anyway, if she was honest, she had to admit that teaching had been one of the dreams, and the others…? Well maybe in another life.

The car stopped, Carolyn applied the hand brake and Rebekka screeched, at the same time banging on the window and waving frantically to the girl in the car that appeared next to them seconds later,

"It's Kylie." She wound the window down, letting in a blast of cold air, "Hi, Kylie."

The girl in the next car got out and smiled at Rebekka. She had long, blond hair and was wearing a jacket made of multicoloured strips of very soft suede attached at only one end like the feathers on a bird, a shiny, silver skirt that just stopped short of indecency, and high, tight fitting boots of the same shining material. Rebekka wound up the window and looked at her own jacket, grey faux fur and exactly what she had wanted until thirty seconds before,

"Oh, God, I'd kill for that jacket…it's fantastic."

She reached for the handle and leapt out of the car,

"Bye, Mum." And she was gone, arm in arm with her new best friend and not a backward glance.

Jake cuffed his brother lightly across the top of the head,

"Come on, Geek, we're here."

James grinned and winked at his mother before joining his brother and several other young people shuffling into the station to catch the train for their school in Ashford seven miles away. Carolyn watched them go and wondered again why schools – or 'Academies of Learning' as they were now called – had abandoned uniforms, though she still had daily battles with Rebekka as she refused to let her go to the extremes of dress that Kylie was allowed for school.

She started the engine and, as she glanced around before reversing, saw Kylie's mother smiling at her from the adjacent car; it was a forced smile that lacked warmth, and Carolyn realised she was returning exactly the same sort of smile. She knew that the family had just moved into one of the houses on the estate of flash, upmarket, executive residences right next door to their lovely old house, and, as far as she and John were concerned, they should never have been built. They were an eyesore and one of the many groups of houses that had been springing up over the years like clusters of ugly red mushrooms, encouraging people to move into the village only because it was easy commuting distance from London. They looked down their noses at the locals and contributed nothing to village life. And now their ancient barns, still bereft of pigs, or even wood-turning equipment (another hobby of John's just waiting for the right time) were overlooked by the new buildings. Infuriating! She felt a little guilty as she knew she could have offered to share the station run with Kylie's mother. But still, both Kylie's parents' businesses were based in London, though they frequently worked from home, so one of them was usually going to the station anyway. She knew this much about them as she received frequent bulletins from Rebekka: 'Kylie's mum has her own beauty business – a chain of shops all over London, and her father is an Architect…Kylie has a purple bedroom…a purple bedroom! Stormin!!'

"Oh, that's nice."

Carolyn gritted her teeth and tried not to let her irritation show when receiving these pieces of information. She had bitten her tongue on hearing the news about the bedroom, just managing to refrain from reminding Rebekka that she had, at some expense, recently finished painting her bedroom and buying new furniture and bedcovers all in white as her daughter had been requesting for the previous six months. In the circumstances she would have found it difficult to befriend Kylie's mum – and she simply did not have the time.

'THE BUBBLE'

She reversed the car then turned towards her school which was only about a mile away from the station taking a few deep breaths as she did so and attempting to compose herself. She knew that, once over the threshold, the day would attack her like a pack of hungry wolves, the only consolation being that there would be no time to think about stroppy teenagers or unwelcome neighbours.

Chapter Three

At the same time as Carolyn Thompson and her children were winding their way along the frosty road to Bartrum station, and John Thompson was enduring the yet-another-Monday-morning-with-a-whole-week-ahead-of-the-same grind to work along the slippery road to Warton, Mervyn Sculley was unlocking the heavy oak door and making his way into the cold, deserted Church at the centre of Middle West Side.

"Blast, I should have left the heating on yesterday," he muttered, blowing on his hands then glancing quickly upwards, embarrassed by the expletive. He went into the vestry and got out the small electric blower, placing it carefully near the pew he always occupied for morning prayers; then, gripping the back of the pew in front of him, lowered himself painfully to his knees.

Alone in a Church so cold that his breath plumed out in little foggy puffs, Mervyn prayed for the state of the world, the local parishes of Upper West Side, Middle West Side and Lower West Side, sick parishioners and the Church both in general and Warton Deanery in particular. He missed Wendy, his wife, who came to these morning sessions with him when she could, but he understood that since Ruth had arrived home from University and was planning to stay for a while, Wendy preferred to make the most of the time she had with her daughter. It was quite understandable.

After half an hour Mervyn got up, switched off the heater, turned out the lights and, locking the door behind him – sad to have to do so, but a sign of the times – walked carefully down the frosty path. Black cloak billowing out behind him, he covered the short distance between the Church and the rectory, his moth eaten woolly gloves providing some protection against the cold, and on his way he passed the grand, old, cream-coloured building that used to be occupied by the Rector and his family many years ago. A beautiful, imposing house, full of character and covered in wisteria, its windows winked in the bright sunlight, smiling benevolently and sympathetically down on the small, red brick construction next door where Mervin and his little family lived.

What different times they must have been when the Church could afford such a place for the Vicar of the Parish, when the Churches themselves were full to bursting, so much so that some had balconies and galleries built to accommodate the crowds thronging through their doors on Sunday mornings. Now fifteen worshippers was considered a good attendance at the one service held on Sunday morning but, as all the members of this small, faithful band were well over sixty and gradually dropping, one by one, Mervin wondered what would happen when they had all fallen off their perches. Still, he wouldn't be around to see it. One year to retirement, just one more year to go.

Cheered by that thought he let himself into the rectory where coffee and toast awaited him.

"I'll walk this mornin' and give the Rector time to finish his breakfast,"

Richard Clegg, the local undertaker, listened for his wife's muffled response from somewhere in the house before shutting the back door carefully behind him and setting off down the path, out of the gate and along the village street towards the rectory to finalise the arrangements for a funeral later that day. 'Time was I knew everyone living on this street,' he mused, 'but now…new houses, new people and everyone rushing off in the mornings to who knows where.' He turned to cross the street and had to wait for nearly five minutes as cars, vans, trucks and lorries all sped past, each one leaving an icy blast in its wake. He stepped out when he thought it was safe, but had to jump smartly out of the path of a speeding car and, looking back, he saw three lads in woolly hats gesturing obscenely at him through the windows. Richard shook his head. 'Time was everybody left their doors unlocked in this village, but you wouldn't do that now, not with characters like that about.' He walked on past the footpath leading down to an orchard and waved at Harry Frost who was making his way towards the river. 'Going to have a look at how much the River Maintenance Authority has hacked into his land when they straightened up the bank last week, I shouldn't wonder.' And with that thought he turned right at the Church towards the Rectory

"Salad for me, mum, with light-as-air-three-bite-melt-in-the-mouth-mini-puffs…but only two"

Decisively, Rebekka held up two fingers of one hand while, with the other, she smoothed her stomach, checking for any signs of excess fat. There were none. Carolyn raised an eyebrow in her daughter's direction that, after a short pause, elicited the desired response.

"…Please."

Jake minced around the room, wiggling his hips and pinching in his waist as he mimicked his sister's voice,

"…and I think I'll have two lettuce leaves, half a carrot stick and a piece of celery with all the fat squeezed out."

"Upstairs now, Jake, half an hour's homework before dinner and leave your sister alone."

Carolyn grabbed Rebekka just in time to stop her from launching herself at her brother and glared at her son; she meant what she said.

Jake stopped mincing and ambled towards the stairs muttering,

"It's ridiculous…why should she eat different food from the rest of us!"

Although she half agreed with him, Carolyn shot him another warning look and he disappeared. She looked at Rebekka while she broke the plastic seals off the lettuce and tomatoes; super slim and determined to stay that way. Well, as long as she carried on eating sensibly, there was no harm in it; in fact she frequently joined her daughter and they ate salads together, leaving the males in the family to their hearty stews.

She looked again at the packet from which she had just tipped the 'hearty stew' and steeled herself against feeling guilty. Of course she would prefer to cook her family's meals from fresh ingredients, but she simply did not have the time. As it was she was worried about not getting the first draft of the governors' report done before she went to bed. It had to be ready by the morning and what with the trouble in the boys' toilets and the totally off-the-wall behaviour of an infant child who had kicked and bitten a teaching assistant then thrown his shoes at one of the other children, she simply had not been able to get it done during the day. She glanced again at Rebekka who was sitting at the breakfast bar casually leafing through what looked like a magazine,

"What's that?" she asked, instantly regretting the question as a travel brochure was waved in her direction with 'SUPER SUMMERS IN FLORIDA' blazoned across the front. Carolyn knew exactly what was coming and it did.

"...Kylie is going to Florida for the whole summer as her parents have a villa there...Kylie says she would go mad if she had to stay in this dead and alive hole during the holidays..."

"Well, we're going to Tenerife for a fortnight," she countered, hoping to stem the flow,

"It's not really the same, though, is it...you know...as having your own villa in Florida...?"

Rebekka's voice tailed off as she noticed her mother's expression and she did have the grace to feel remorseful. She knew that her parents had saved for their holiday.

"Actually, mum, Tenerife will be good."

"Yes, of course it will. And it'll probably be the last time your brothers will want to come on holiday with us."

Rebekka looked up with an exaggeratedly 'happy' face,

"Well, what do you know? There's always a bright side to everything. Roll on next year!" And mother and daughter laughed together, an uncomfortable moment successfully averted but, secretly, Carolyn still felt niggled. The grass was always greener...villas abroad nowadays were the norm, and it wasn't just the young people. More and more retired couples spent the summer in one of the West Sides and then wintered in Florida, Spain or Italy. No wonder she hardly knew anyone in the village any more.

At eleven thirty that evening Carolyn Thompson sat in the armchair opposite her husband who was already asleep, his glasses falling off the end of his nose and the newspaper in a crumpled heap on the floor where it had fallen. She took a sip of the brandy she had poured herself as a reward for almost finishing the governors' report and rubbed her eyes, exhausted. She would finish it early tomorrow morning before Kieran had a chance to throw any more wobblies; and providing, of course, that the boys could use their toilets without succumbing to the temptation of stuffing them full of paper towels. Yes, tomorrow…more of the same.

She didn't know it, but tomorrow wouldn't be the same; in fact nothing would ever be the same again.

'THE BUBBLE'

Chapter Four

Barry Munden, dressed as usual in clean shirt, grey trousers and silk tie underneath immaculate white coat and striped apron, pulled up the blinds and looked out at the traffic already rushing along the road past his shop in the centre of Middle West Side. He was the only butcher left now to provide meat for all three villages, but it was enough as most of the newcomers seemed to shop in the towns after work; still, the old folk continued to want fresh meat which Barry was happy to go on providing for as long as he could. He opened the door and inhaled the frosty air, sharp and cold against his skin. He looked down the street towards the river gleaming in the distance. Time was he could remember when there were more than fifty shops altogether in the three villages, four of them butchers, and they all made a good living as everyone wanted fresh produce in those days.

The sun shone brightly on the river and Barry wondered if it would freeze. Time was when the river froze every year and people from all three villages had great fun on the ice, skating parties…competitions…all sharing their food and drink with each other. Oh well, times change. Folk are too busy for that sort of thing these days, even if the river did freeze, which it hadn't for many years now.

Barry closed the door against the cold and went inside. As it was only eight o'clock he didn't really expect any customers for at least another half an hour; time to get a cup of tea and a piece of toast to set him up for the morning.

If he had stayed at his door, or even in the shop, for a little longer he would have noticed the traffic come to a sudden halt. He may have thought nothing of it, just a temporary hold up of the sort that continually caused so much frustration to the motorists who all apparently needed urgently to be elsewhere. He would have had no way of knowing, at this point, what had occurred on the boundaries of all three villages. Over in the Church Reverend Sculley lowered himself to his knees to pray as usual, also unaware of the phenomenon that was about to change their lives forever.

"What is it now, mum, why have you stopped?"

"Because the cars in front of me have stopped, Jake," Carolyn measured out her words carefully, trying not to let her frustration show, but dammit, she had no hope now of finishing that dratted report. Still nothing moved. She revved the engine, pointlessly, but at least it drowned out the sound of Rebekka tutting. Then she noticed that people were getting out of their cars. Oh dear, must be an accident. Some poor souls…

A woman in a pale woollen coat and white scarf was running down the line of cars, stopping to talk briefly to each driver who then got out and began to walk towards the front of the queue.

"What's happening?"

Rebekka leaned forward and watched as the woman spoke to the driver of the white car directly in front of them.

"I think there must have been an accident and people are going to see…"

Before Carolyn had the chance to tell her children that **they** would **not** be going to stare ghoulishly at some poor devils, bleeding and in a state of shock, sitting at the roadside, the woman's face appeared at her window. Carolyn wound it down,

"What's happened?"

"We don't know…it's extraordinary…we just can't get through…I can't explain…go and see…"

She spoke rapidly, gasping for air and obviously in a state of shock.

"But…what…?"

Before Carolyn could finish her question, the woman had dashed off to the car behind.

"What did she say, mum"?

"What did she mean…?"

'THE BUBBLE'

Jake and Rebekka were both leaning forward and even James had removed his ear piece and was staring at the line of cars ahead of them.

"I have no idea, but we'd better go and have a look."

Carolyn switched off the engine, then all four of them got out of the car and walked forward to join the throng of people making their way to the head of the queue. The car at the front was an old and very ordinary dark blue estate, the same model that Carolyn and John had had before the children persuaded them they needed a Motion Wagon, the very latest thing – and, of course, almost exactly the same as the one Kylie's mum had got the year before. They looked around and could see no reason why the car could not go forward. There was nothing at all in the way.

"Oh, this is ridiculous!"

They carried on walking and noticed that the other people on foot were all behind or level with the blue car. Some had ventured off the road and were making their way across the fields in both directions, but still in line with the blue car. The atmosphere was strangely still and silent, the frosty air punctuated by the occasional cries of, 'what's happened…?' 'What is it…?', but as no-one had an answer, everyone just kept walking and staring…then leaning…

As they got closer to the blue car, Carolyn and the children noticed that people were banging their fists on something. They were poking, prodding and then leaning their whole weight on what appeared to be an invisible barrier just in front of the blue car and stretching out from it on either side. They explored it with their hands, reminding Carolyn, as she watched, of a mime artist she had seen many years before pretending he was in a box, his hands skilfully marking out its boundaries. One or two people giggled hysterically as no-one could believe what they were seeing – or not seeing!

Curious to know more, James walked forward and rested his hands against the apparently invisible wall. It felt like rubber, a sort of hard, plastic coated rubber, slightly oily to the touch, but it was completely invisible. Looking through it he could see the road and fields on the other side. He took his hands away, rubbing them slowly on his trousers. This could not be happening; it simply could not be happening.

"What the 'ell's goin' on?"

The three woolly-hatted lads from the car that had made Richard Clegg leap for the pavement the day before were now loping towards the barrier, their shouted enquiry addressed to no-one in particular. They stopped at the invisible wall and banged on it with their fists. The tallest one of the three, a lad called Kevin, butted it as though it were a football, and then rubbed his head, grinning sheepishly. Simon, short, thickset and obviously the leader of the three, stuck his hands in his pockets and beckoned the other two with a sharp flick of his head. He muttered something and indicated their car, a small, red, shabby looking vehicle parked someway down the line. Jason, the third lad, gave a bark of laughter,

"Yeah, nice one, Si. Let's do it. Someone's gotta sort this out. It ain't real."

They ambled back to their car, kicking at the frosted tufts of grass as they went. A few moments later the crowd of people, still frozen in a state of total shock and believing that things would revert to normal in a few minutes and that there was, of course, a completely rational explanation that would soon have them all laughing, were further traumatised by the sight of a shabby red car speeding past all the others and ramming with great force into the invisible barrier. There were gasps of horror as it rebounded and swung round, the back of it slamming into the stationary blue car. The three lads got out, visibly shaken but trying hard to keep up the air of bravado. Jason's nose was bleeding and Kevin had a cut on his head.

"You bloody idiots! What the hell did you think you were doing?"

It was the owner of the blue car, the local publican on his way to the Mega Store for supplies. The sudden noise of the crash had the effect of galvanising everyone into action. The wall that the lads had obviously thought they could break by crashing their car through it had held as though made of the toughest steel known to man, and suddenly people started to run as fast as they could away from it and back towards their cars. Many paused for long enough to try and use their mobile phones, but were further alarmed to discover they couldn't get a signal.

"It's dead…nothing,"

Carolyn threw the useless phone back into her bag,

"Quick, get in the car. We've got to get back to the village…see if there's another way out."

They joined the mad exodus of cars reversing onto the fields then speeding back the way they had come only half an hour before. They passed Kylie and her mum, and Rebekka made a gesture of hopelessness which she knew wouldn't prevent them from going on to see for themselves why everyone was going the wrong way at this time in the morning.

By lunch time the mood in the three villages of Upper West Side, Middle West Side and Lower West Side was one of profound shock and disbelief. The mobile phones would not work at all; the house phones worked but only if the calls were being made to someone in one of the three villages. People were out on the streets trying to make sense of something that made no sense at all. It appeared that the invisible barrier formed a perfect circle around the three villages. How far up did it go? There was no way of knowing as, staring upwards, everything appeared normal; the sun was shining and clouds were moving across a sky that was as blue and untroubled as it had been all morning. Did the barrier meet above their heads? Were they encapsulated in a sort of dome? Would night fall as usual?

"…and if we are in a dome, how long before the air runs out?"

Carolyn glared at the speaker. That sort of remark was not helpful when many people were already on the verge of hysteria, the only thing holding them back being the profound belief that it wasn't really happening. Somehow, possibly by the morning, this strange thing would have disappeared and they could all get on with their lives – probably get their fifteen minutes of fame as they tried to describe it to the television people who would, of course, want to know why they had all stayed at home on 11th January 2020.

Standing in the street with everyone else, Carolyn clung to John's arm. She had felt weak with relief when she had seen him pulling up in their drive five minutes after she and the children had arrived home. If there was some sort of barrier thank God he was on the same side of it as she was. She felt sure she could face pretty well anything if they were together. What she didn't know at this point was that nobody who belonged in any of the three villages had been left stranded on the other side of the wall. There were people away on holiday who were missing, but everyone, without exception, who was expecting to sleep in one of the West Sides that night would do so. John hadn't had the time or inclination yet to try and explain to Carolyn the strange compulsion that had forced him to turn the car and head for home before he had got even half way to Warton. He had tried to resist, but no amount of reasoning was powerful enough to stop him from turning the car round. It was only when he had reached home that Carolyn had told him about the wall and he had gone to see for himself. He had gone back through Upper West Side towards Warton, but could only get as far as the boundary before he met the wall, a wall that hadn't been there much earlier that morning.

Although the pavements were full of people standing around, huddled together in groups, an eerie stillness hung over the whole street. The naturally garrulous were stupefied into silence while others spoke in whispers as though it was a holy place or they were in the presence of death. Some tried to reassure, '...it'll be gone by morning, you'll see...' while others strode from group to group, needing to talk. A few of the old ladies from the row of ancient cottages in the lane had come up to the main road where they stood together looking frightened and thinking of their grandchildren.

Carolyn glanced across to where Rebekka and Kylie were standing clinging to each other, and Kylie's mum nodded in her direction. She too was clinging to her husband and their faces, like those of everyone else, were white and tense with shock. Many people were still trying their mobile phones, seeing them as a lifeline and believing that there would be a sudden break through and they would again be in contact with those on the other side of the wall.

Around four o'clock the sun set as usual for a bright day in January and the light slowly gave way to twilight. It was all so normal that many were tempted back to the barrier, convinced that it must have lifted. But it hadn't; not then and not the following morning when, after a sleepless night, the residents of the West Sides all rushed to the village boundaries forming a weird, curved line as they once again prodded, poked and leaned against the invisible wall.

A few took photographs of each other, still convinced that, like ice on the river, the barrier would disappear and their photographs would be eagerly seized by the media. As there was nothing to see, the obstruction being more transparent than the cleanest glass ever produced and totally non-reflective, the keenest photographers encouraged their friends and families to place both hands against it, moving their feet as far away as possible to let the wall support their full weight. When they were subsequently to explain this phenomenon to anyone who hadn't experienced it, they wanted to show beyond doubt that the wall had been there.

On Friday morning John drove out to the village boundary and was back ten minutes later,

"Still there?"

"Yes."

Carolyn continued to load the dishwasher; James was staring out of the window, Rebekka announced she was going round to see Kylie and the loud music emanating from the direction of his room told Carolyn where Jake was. Everyone was trying to keep things as normal as possible in a situation that was as far from normal as they had ever experienced. They walked about as though treading on egg shells, fearful of what may happen next, but reluctant to share their fears. Would the water supply suddenly dry up? What about electricity and gas? So far these things were available as usual. There was no problem with food as the Thompsons were living out of the freezer and on Thursday Carolyn had gone to the local shop for the first time and found that she could buy bread and milk. But for how long? With a totally incomprehensible, invisible, rubbery barrier cutting them off from the rest of the world how long could they survive? It was the question uppermost in everyone's mind but the question they were all reluctant to address. It had only been four days; it would surely go away. It had to.

That night the sky was clear, lit by a thousand stars and bathed in the glow from a moon so bright it silvered the river and danced on frosted grass. It shone on Harry Frost's ploughed fields making burnished steel of the turned earth; it picked out the hen coop in 'mad' Martha's yard; and in her orchard, down near the river, it threw the branches of the apple trees against the sky so sharply that every twig was visible, delicate veins against a sky of skin. And from one of these trees a young man lowered himself to the ground, so softly that his feet made no more sound than the falling of a stray autumn leaf. He stood for a moment before padding lightly across the grass and disappearing up the road towards Middle West Side. From an upstairs window Martha saw him arrive and nodded silently as she watched him go.

Chapter Five

On Saturday evening the men in Middle West Side decided it was time for action. Many more of them than usual had crowded into the bars at The Rose and Crown and, over more pints of beer than they were accustomed to, concluded that the situation was ridiculous. 'Enough is enough,' they shouted, banging their pint pots down on the bar. Whatever it was that was stopping them from getting out of the three villages had to be tackled – and now! They telephoned The Hat and Feathers in Lower West Side and then The Green Man in Upper West Side and all were agreed that they would meet at the wall on the road leading to Bartrum the following morning.

And so it was that on Sunday morning at nine o'clock most of the men from the three villages had gathered on the fields along the wall near the point where the road, if they could get any further, would take them to Bartrum. The assortment of vehicles, farm machinery and tools they had brought with them lent an air of festivity to the scene as if they were setting up for an agricultural show, though the absence of bunting and the expressions on the men's faces would soon have led the casual observer to realise that something more serious was afoot. If that failed, then the sight of Gordon Golightly, striding, shouting and pointing would have dispelled any lingering doubts.

Gordon was tall and solidly built with a mass of thick, dark hair that curled down over his collar. A very successful lawyer, he lived in the largest, grandest house in Middle West Side. In his mid fifties and contemplating retirement, he had been gradually taking on less and less work; after all, it was not as though he really needed to work and the life of self appointed squire suited him very nicely. He had been Chairman of the Parish Council for the past five years, not because he was particularly altruistic, or possessed of great leadership skills, but he shouted a lot and relied on intimidating others to get his own way. If he was going to stay in Middle West Side, he'd damn well make sure it was a place fit to live in, give those johnnies at the Borough what for if they didn't fall in line.

'THE BUBBLE'

Gordon Golightly didn't take kindly to anything that got in his way, and this damned wall would be no exception. He spoke with authority and others listened, not daring to doubt that he was right.

David Gibbons, the local haulage contractor, jumped down from his lorry and walked up to two of the men standing staring at the place where they knew the wall to be,

"Rum do this and no mistake." He said, shaking his head.

"I've lived here all me life and never known nothing like it," replied Brian Harris, one of several builders who lived in the three villages.

"It's a bugger…just nothing there to see, yet we can't get through."

Ernie Briggs, the third man in the group spoke last. He ran a small car repair business and thought he had come across every material known to man, but never an invisible wall as tough as steel.

"OK everyone listen up, please."

As Gordon prepared to address the assembled company through a loud hailer, he looked round, the epitome of country gentleman in a tweed jacket with matching cap, and waited for silence, playing the part of squire very well.

"I thought his type went out with the last century," muttered David, glaring at the man standing in front of them all. He couldn't stand Gordon as he was sure that there had been something going on between him and his wife, Jane, a couple of years ago, but Jane had denied it and he had never been able to prove anything. They had stayed together, but he couldn't help wondering…and he hated the type anyway, smooth sod. Gordon threw him a look that clearly indicated he was waiting for silence from everyone, including him, and David looked back, not bothering to hide his contempt. Gordon turned away; he knew exactly why David was regarding him with undisguised loathing and cared not a jot. The 'thing' with Jane Gibbons had been brief and not particularly memorable, certainly not worth pursuing to the extent of risking what he had with Claudia, his own beautiful, dark-haired wife. Now she was a catch for any man, even without the money that had enabled them to buy The Manor.

Yes, the local haulage contractor was welcome to his woman, dark-haired like Claudia and certainly a gocr between the sheets, but...well frankly...more than a little bit of a tart. Best leave that well alone in the future. So back to the business in hand. Gordon raised the loud hailer again,

"We'll do this systematically...chain saw first if you please, Harris."

Brian stepped forward, started the saw and approached the wall very carefully, not knowing how it would react on contact with the mystery material. His arm jerked as the whirling blade touched the barrier but he held it steady and watched in complete astonishment as the teeth of the saw, normally sharp enough to cut a year's supply of logs, were, in a few moments, ground down to nothing. The wall remained unchanged. Brian switched off and turned slowly round, holding up his saw so that everyone could see what had happened.

"Well, bugger me..."

Ernie scratched his head and looked at his mate's now completely useless blade.

"I put that in yesterday...brand new it was..."

Brian threw it down in disgust.

"Well, pity about that Harris. Now Gibbons and all the rest of you chaps with lorries back up to the wall and apply pressure...and you," Gordon turned to the owner of the only cherry picker in the village, "...you go up as high as you can...see if you can find out if this blessed thing has a top to it."

Gordon barked out his orders and for the rest of the day the men from the three villages tried their best to break the wall. They jabbed at it with anything they could find and even bombarded it with a huge demolition ball; they moved around to the boundaries of the other villages, hoping to find a weak spot but without any success. Finally Ernie Briggs had a go at it with his new laser, the pride and joy of his tool collection, but it made no difference. Nothing made any impression at all on this strange, unknown substance forming an impenetrable barrier around them.

Tired and dispirited, the men threw themselves and their tools down on the grass at the end of the day and sat around shaking their heads in complete bewilderment. Unaccustomed to being beaten by anything or anybody, Gordon Golightly was particularly annoyed; he looked up into a darkening sky and saw birds wheeling about above his head as usual. They hadn't been able to find a top to this 'wall,' but there must be one and if birds were about, where were the aircraft? Always around making a racket overhead and disturbing the peace when you didn't want them, but where were they when you needed them? Surely that would be the way…when the rest of the country discovered that all the inhabitants of The West Sides were missing they'd send in the helicopters to find out what was going on. He looked towards the wall…and, of course, they could raise the alarm by signalling to anyone trying to get **into** The West Sides…though…strange now come to think of it… although they had been on the boundaries all day no-one had come towards the wall from the other side. All the same a watch should be mounted. There was a need to be organised. And with that thought he raised the loud hailer to his mouth again,

"Right everyone listen up one more time…"

David Gibbons let out his breath very slowly and raised himself up on one elbow, at the same time muttering venomously to Ernie and Brian,

"If he shouts through that thing once more I'm going to ram it down his throat."

Unaware of the fate that could possibly await him, Gordon addressed the crowd for the last time that day,

"You've all done well, but we're batting our heads against a wall here," he paused, but there was no laughter, not even a smile. Clearing his throat he continued,

"I think we should all go home now and get some sleep. I am calling a meeting for Monday morning at nine o'clock on Middle West Side School playing field. If it's raining we'll re-schedule but I think it has to be outside as we should get most of the people from the three villages, and there's no other space big enough. I shall speak to the Chairmen of the other two Parish Councils and get them to come along. We'll hold a joint meeting and try to come up with a plan of action."

As they made their way home the men couldn't wait to tell their wives and partners about the proposed meeting which caused almost as much astonishment as the wall itself; it was the first time the three villages had done anything together in living memory.

Chapter Six

"It's easy to see why they've never collaborated before," Caroline murmured as she stood in the middle of the school playing field on Monday morning with John and the children. It had started quite well with Gordon Golightly taking the lead, of course, and introducing the other two men on the platform with him. On his left sat Clive Simpson, small and almost bald, an accountant by profession, who had been Chairman of Lower West Side Council for nearly three years. On his right was Peter Cunningham, quite a rough looking character with wild, greying hair and a tanned complexion, weathered from running a nursery in Upper West Side for most of his working life. He had been Chair of that Council for less than a year, though he had wanted the position for longer, and was determined to prove himself. Petty jealousies between the Councils went back years and each man was determined, in his own way, to fight his corner.

Everyone was there, of course, apart from the very old and very ill, as there was nowhere else to go, and, looking round, Carolyn noticed that the inhabitants of each of The West Sides had divided themselves neatly so that they were standing opposite their own Chairman, and similarly, the Council members of each Parish were clustered together, standing just below where their respective Chairmen were sitting. There were, and always had been, internal wrangles, and most of the inhabitants of each West Side had no time for these little bureaucrats who, as far as they could see, did no good whatsoever, but at times like this showing solidarity with one's own was important.

Gordon was pontificating, outlining the need to keep a round the clock watch on the wall and send a message back to the villages as soon as there was any sign of it disintegrating. He would, of course, be the spokesman on behalf of all three villages to deal with the media interest that would follow the disappearance of the wall…with his experience of legal matters he would be able to exert the kind of control needed to prevent them all from being exploited…

He paused,

"...there will of course be money to be made that could benefit us all." He smiled at the assembled company,

"Benefit him more like," Ernie whispered to Brian.

"Er...Mr. Chair, if I may interject..." Clive Simpson cleared his throat and tentatively took possession of the microphone. Gordon had rung several people earlier that morning, including Ernie, Brian and David, and bullied them into arriving on the field at half past six to erect a platform and run cables from the school to operate a sound system with microphone attached. David had gone, grudgingly, declaring to Jane that it was worth it to stop Gordon from yelling at everyone again through that blessed loud hailer. Gordon had also made sure that he and his two colleagues had chairs to sit on. Too bad about everyone else...they would have to stand...too much trouble to get chairs out for all of them...there wouldn't be enough anyway. Gordon turned and looked impatiently at Clive; he regarded him as a peculiar, insignificant little man who he had never really had much time for. Allowed his councillors to run rings round him, by all accounts. Clive continued,

"I think keeping a watch is all very well, but should we not perhaps form several committees to deal with well..." His voice tailed off as he tried to imagine what in this new and unfamiliar world they would be dealing with. Peter Cunningham reached across the table in front of Gordon and grabbed the microphone,

"It seems to me that all the committees under the sun ain't going to make any difference to the fact that we're all prisoners 'ere. We can't get further than the edges of each village and, as far as we can make out, in nearly a week, nobody ain't bothered to try and get in. We're stuck and that's the truth of it. I'm sorry, Mr Chairman, but I believe in saying it like it is."

'Oh, you odious man,' Gordon thought as he reached for the microphone, but before he could attempt to pick up the threads of the meeting again and get back onto some kind of track, all hell broke loose.

"He's right, he's right," yelled the villagers from Upper West Side in support of their Chairman then everyone started talking at once. Angry voices rang out in the cold air and people stamped on the frosty grass to try and keep warm. The other villagers joined in; there was a need to find someone to blame, and as their three Chairmen had put themselves up there, they may as well let them have it. One woman's voice rang out above the rest as she raised her fist in the air,

"Let's face it, we're all going to die! There will be no water, gas, electricity or even air to breathe before very long and we've had it...we've had it..." She broke down and started to sob at which point several others joined in and the voices again rose to a crescendo.

Nobody saw where he came from but, while Gordon tried in vain to restore order, a young man appeared at the side of the platform where he stood quietly and waited. Gradually, as people became aware of his presence, the noise subsided. Gordon, not seeing the young man, thought the silence was, as always, due to his powers of control, and ran his hand through his thick, wavy hair while preparing to continue. The young man cleared his throat and Gordon looked round,

"Excuse me...if I may..."

The young man stepped towards the table and Gordon looked as though he had been struck,

"No, I'm afraid you may not, whoever you are. This is a meeting, now please return to the floor..."

"Oh shut up Gordon, for Gawd's sake and let him speak. You may as well, I've heard farts that make more sense than you have so far today. This is not one of your Council Meetings and the 'floor' you may have noticed is a frosty field. We are all in this together and we need all the help we can get, wherever it comes from."

The raucous voice that cut through the air, loudly and clearly enough for all to hear without the aid of a microphone, belonged to Jane Gibbons; next to her, David's face broke into a smile that spread slowly across his face. There were sniggers from everywhere and Jake dissolved into such a severe fit of the giggles that James had to dig him in the ribs to shut him up. Gordon tried, unsuccessfully, to hide his fury as he turned his head slowly to where the young man was standing.

"And you are?"

"Jack…just call me Jack."

Well…Jack…I'm sure we are all interested to know what you have to say to us."

On Gordon's lips the newcomer's name sounded like an insult, while the supercilious expression on his face together with the coldness of his tone made it clear that the opposite was true; he wasn't remotely interested in anything the young man might say. Standing together in the middle of the field, Rebekka and Kylie who had, up to this point, been bored by the meeting, nudged each other and suddenly became very interested in what was taking place on the platform. Jack stepped forward and looked slowly round at the crowd of people before him. He smiled, and as he did so the day suddenly felt a little warmer, everywhere looked just a touch brighter in the January sunshine. Jack wasn't tall, he wasn't dark and he wasn't even handsome in the accepted sense of the word. Slightly built, he stood about five foot eight with light brown curly hair, blue eyes and the most engaging smile imaginable.

He cleared his throat again and started to speak,

"Ladies and gentlemen, it seems to me that one of the things we should be doing to try and deal with the situation in which we find ourselves is to examine our assets,"

"He can examine my assets any time," Kylie whispered. Rebekka nudged her friend and glanced quickly towards Carolyn, hoping her mum hadn't heard as she knew how much she disapproved of Kylie's overwhelming interest in boys. Jack continued,

"We have, I believe, still got electricity, gas and water, even though it seems these amenities have suddenly become selective about what they will power. We have washing machines, but no televisions and our computers are not working."

"How do you know that nobody else's TV or PC is working? It might just be yours,"

a voice shouted from the crowd, then one or two others, emboldened by his example joined in,

"...Yeah... and what about when everything runs out? What then, eh?"

"...And what about food...?

"...and money? What are we supposed to do about money?"

"...Everything will soon get cut off when we don't pay our bills."

"...You're living in cuckoo land, mate!"

. Jack spoke again,

"No, I'm living right here, the same as the rest of you, and at the moment we have no choice about that. When – or if – resources start to run out then we deal with the problems that will present. At the moment we must work with what we have, our survival depends on it. I think we should all go to our homes and look at what we've got; perhaps try and think of ways in which we can make use of everything around, come up with ideas for maximising all the resources available to us at present; then it would be useful to hold another meeting, say in a week's time, see where we've all got to," He paused and turned to Gordon, "In case of rain, perhaps we could use the ballroom at The Manor House, Mr. Golightly"

He waited as Gordon blustered. He had no intention of allowing this rabble, this bunch of oiks, to trample through his house and ruin his ballroom floor,

"Er...well...truth is, you see it's...er...having...er...the floor's being stripped at the moment and the chandeliers are down for cleaning," (which, of course, wasn't the truth at all, but the best he could come up with on the spur of the moment.) Jack waited and Gordon continued,

"But look, there's no reason why we shouldn't use my barn. It's plenty big enough and more than half empty at this time of year."

And so it was agreed that everyone would go away and do as Jack suggested, then meet again in exactly a week, unless anything else earth-shattering happened in the mean time. Jack turned to go but, determined to try and have the last word, Gordon looked towards him, at the same time addressing everyone on the field.

"I was, of course, going to make a similar suggestion to yours if I'd had half a chance, but no matter. And it's all very well taking up your idea, but it seems to me that we have still ignored the main issue which is how to get rid of a totally unnatural, invisible wall. We simply cannot accept that we are all prisoners and go about as if nothing was wrong; we can't make lives here without any contact with the outside world, it's just not possible!"

Feeling sure he had well and truly trumped the intruder, Gordon faced the crowd waiting for applause, or, at the very least murmurs of agreement. Oh yes, he'd bring them all back to reality. But there was silence, then Jack spoke again.

"I don't think we have any choice other than to accept the situation as it is at present." There was a long pause and he stepped right to the front of the platform, once again looking slowly around at the crowd who were giving him their undivided attention; he continued,

"Meanwhile, maybe we could try and do something about the other invisible walls in our midst."

The silence was almost tangible as everyone looked first at the people standing next to them and then at the obvious gaps which had been left between the inhabitants of each West Side. A few even smiled across the gaps at people they vaguely recognised and Jack quietly left the stage.

Carolyn linked arms with John as they made their way towards the gate,

"Well, that was interesting; I wonder who he is, that Jack, and where he lives. He certainly made a lot of sense." She giggled, "It was great to see Gordon Golightly cut down to size at last."

"Yes," John was thoughtful, "But Jack didn't have a go or anything, he just sort of let Gordon trip himself up. Oh well, let's go home and see what we can come up with; as the man says, there isn't really an alternative which, in some ways, makes life easier."

Gordon Golightly shouted even more than usual at the men who were helping him to take the sound system apart and dismantle the platform. Damned little whipper-snapper! Who the hell was he and what right did he have to poke his nose in where it wasn't wanted? Gordon would have had difficulty admitting it, even to himself, but it was the fact that everyone did seem to want the stranger's intervention and subsequent advice that really riled him. Suddenly he was struck by such an extraordinary thought that it stopped him in his tracks. He stood stock still, clutching a speaker, and wondered how a young man he had never seen before in his life knew that he had a ballroom at the Manor big enough for a large crowd of people.

Simon, Kevin and Jason jostled towards the entrance of the field along with everyone else. Once on the pavement and when there was hardly anyone else left, Kevin nudged Simon, his face breaking into the idiot grin that the other two had grown accustomed to over the years,

"'Ere, Si…Jase, look what I've got. I nicked 'em." He produced half a dozen mobile phones from his pocket and held them out for his friends to see.

Simon looked at him and slowly shook his head,

"Do you know, Kev, I worry about you, I really do; if you 'ad a brain you'd be dangerous"

Chapter Seven

That evening Jane Gibbons was serving up dinner as usual while David sat with his arms resting on the table and waited. Only this evening, instead of reading the paper, because of course there wasn't one, he was staring at his wife and smiling.

"What?" She half smiled back as she placed a plate of food in front of him then turned to fetch her own, but was prevented from doing so as David gently held her wrist and looked at her in a way that made her giggle.

"What?"

"I'm proud of you, that's what, standing up to Gordon the Gorgon like you did."

"Oh him." She reclaimed her wrist and went to fetch her plate, glad that she was able to turn away from her husband for a few moments. She had to be sure that she could compose her expression into one of complete indifference before she went back to the table. She loathed Gordon Golightly, but David was no fool; there would be no reason to hate him as she did, had she not once felt so infatuated by the man that she had risked losing everything. How could she have been so stupid when he had treated her like dirt. Thank God she had come to her senses before it was too late.

She sat down at the table. How could she have fallen for the classic lines '…Claudia was frigid…Claudia didn't even begin to understand him…he was going to leave Claudia…' And then, of course, when she had seen them together at the New Year's Eve Ball she had known at once how it really was. Claudia had Gordon twisted right round her little finger, she had only to beckon and he was right there ready to do whatever she wanted. She had watched him fawning all over his wife, dancing attendance to her every whim and carefully, oh so carefully, avoiding looking in her direction as she had sat, not at the top table with his party of course, but further down the room with David and their friends. She had sensed his nervousness when his eyes had strayed towards her for a moment and the message was loud and clear – you are nothing, this is my real life. She was so besotted with him and still so much in need of reassurance that she would have been happy with a wink and a smile, something which said, 'I have to do this, but what I have with you is what matters,' but it clearly wasn't. He had treated her like a fool, reduced her to nothing and it was then she had started hating him. Gordon loved money and Claudia had it, lots of it; that was his passion and, when she had seen him in his true colours, her passion for him had turned to loathing.

He had come sniffing round again, of course, thinking everything could go on as before with his 'bit on the side,' and Jane had had the satisfaction of telling him where to get off, well 'off' had certainly been the second word she had used! She smiled at the memory of his face, maybe no-one had ever told him to do that before.

She and David were OK, in fact they were more than OK; compared with her first husband, Stuart, David was a rock and she had been a fool to risk losing him. She wasn't really one to analyse situations, but she realised that David's long hours at work had left her feeling lonely and neglected. It was a familiar story which didn't really excuse her behaviour, but as the boys were spending more time with their father these days she had suddenly felt very alone and in need of reassurance. Enter Gordon with his smooth talk and dark good looks, just when she had been at her most vulnerable. Still it was over, no harm done and her marriage was still intact. She smiled as she heard her boys, Sam and Nick, arguing in their room, and for the thousandth time felt so grateful that when the wall came they were on her side of it – and David hadn't been away on one of his long hauls. If she had to be trapped, at least she was trapped with the three most precious men in her life.

David suddenly reached out and took her hand,

"Are you afraid?" he asked.

She put down her fork and thought for a moment.

"I don't know…I don't think so, but I think I should be, if you know what I mean."

He smiled,

"Yes, I do know what you mean. I feel the same. It's like it's still not really happening…like a joke or something. You know in a minute someone's going to jump out of a hedge and say we've been tricked, filmed for the telly, and we're going to get a lot of money if we let them show it. And we're all going to be laughing and everything will go back to normal."

"Yeah, that's right. I'm just so glad you and the boys are here."

"Yeah. I'll bet Stuart's doing his nut, though," David said, echoing Jane's thoughts of a few minutes before and they both laughed.

Carolyn and John sat sipping their brandies by the fire in Holly Tree House, swirling the golden liquid around in their glasses and staring through it at the flames licking over the logs; the children were asleep and the house was quiet. Neither of them could remember when they had last done this and, having talked endlessly about 'the situation,' they were now peacefully lost in their own thoughts, disturbed only by the crackle and hiss from the grate. As they hadn't bothered to get up and switch on any lights they were bathed in the warm glow from the fire while flickering shadows danced on the ceiling.

"It's surreal, isn't it?" Carolyn murmured, glancing towards her husband, "We're so used to a world where we have to find answers to any problems that arise…there are always answers…only not this time. And here we sit, sipping our brandies, because there is absolutely nothing we can do. But why aren't we panicking, leaping up and down, screaming…?"

John laughed,

"Would it help if we did?"

And Carolyn smiled,

"No, of course not, but you know what I mean. It's like that French expression, 'the more things change the more they stay the same.' Everything has changed, but at this moment everything feels the same."

"Only it isn't is it?"

"No, it isn't."

They were silent again until John leaned forward,

"Caro, do you remember that time we were snowed in, when the children were little…?"

"Oh, yes I do! We couldn't get out and no-one could get into the village for nearly a week, and we made bread and soup and went round to make sure all the old ladies were OK. Do you remember…we wrapped up in our warm clothes and went for long walks; you made a sledge for the children and everyone got together and we all skated on the river one evening…we had hot soup, sausages and baked potatoes and those two brothers Vic and Jim played their violins. We all stayed out laughing and singing until well after dark…We felt so alive somehow, during that week"

Carolyn's eyes were shining in the firelight. John spoke softly,

"Do you remember what we said when the snow melted and we all got back to normal?"

Carolyn looked at him,

"Yes, I do. We said it had been the best time any of us could ever remember."

Nearby, in one of the largest, most ostentatious houses that formed part of the new development of executive residences, Kylie O'Dell was trying not to listen to the sound of her parents arguing. Well, strictly speaking, the sound of her mother arguing with step father number two. She couldn't remember living with her real father as she had only been eighteen months old when her mother had left him for a new man, the love of her life, who had lasted precisely five years; long enough for Patti to marry and then ditch him for Giles O'Dell, who very quickly became husband number three. There was that to be said for Patti; she always married her man and she and Kylie both took his name, because, of course, it was always for keeps. She sat hugging her knees as her mother's voice rang through the house,

‘THE BUBBLE’

“Giles, I will go mad, stark, staring mad if we cannot get beyond these three villages. It’s insane, absolutely insane and something must be done!”

“Yes, of course, thank-you for that, darling, I’m sure nobody else has thought of it. What shall we do? Perhaps we could write to someone, or telephone? That’s it! We’ll telephone and write only, in case you hadn’t noticed, there is no chance of letters getting beyond the wall and the phones can’t reach the other side either. Oh, I know, we’ll email! No, silly me…forgot for a moment…that isn’t working either and the wall is apparently impenetrable. But you’re right as always, Patti, something must be done!”

“There’s no need to be sarcastic; it doesn’t help.”

“And neither, my darling, does your hysterical ranting so unless you can stop stating the obvious and come out with something useful, for crying out loud…SHUT UP!”

Kylie flinched at the sound of a door banging and reached for the purple duvet, wrapping it round her and curling up even more tightly. She wished she had a brother to talk to, or even a sister like Bekks, yes Bekks was nice and always made her feel good. Kylie knew her friend was envious of the things she had: the clothes, the ultra smart home, her long, blond hair and the holidays in Florida. She basked in her friend’s admiration; it made her feel better and for a while she even believed it all herself. Of course she was lucky, and, seeing herself in her friend’s eyes, she was for a short time able to forget the loneliness and the pain.

Down the lane a little further along the road, Hilda Bates and Florence Wrenn sat together in unfamiliar proximity either side of the gas fire that hissed and popped in the tiny sitting room of Number One, The Cottages. Florence fidgeted and scarcely stopped talking for long enough to draw breath; while Hilda, draining the last dregs of her cocoa, was beginning to regret her impulsive decision to knock on her neighbour’s door and suggest they spend the evening together. It was not something they usually did and now Hilda remembered why.

'THE BUBBLE'

"Oh dear, oh dear....I don't know...I really don't know. What a to-do and no mistake...what a to-do."

Florence fiddled with a tissue, blew her nose, tucked the tissue away up her sleeve, tied the paisley scarf she always wore around her head more firmly at the nape of her neck, pulled down her jumper then picked at the material of her trousers with tiny, sharp jabs like a bird pecking seed. Everything about her was bird-like from her slight frame to the quick, darting movements, so much so that people often thought her surname, which was genuine, must be a nickname.

Hilda, on the other hand was comfortable; large hips spread to fill her favourite fireside chair, thighs fitted snugly together under the wool skirt from which dimpled knees and plump legs protruded, crossed at the ankles with surprisingly small feet snuggled into fluffy slippers. Her white hair was always coiled on top of her head and usually tucked into one of the hats she wore, summer and winter, whatever the weather. Hilda laughed a lot, and when she did her whole face lit up, sparkling eyes and white teeth radiating an infectious inner joy. For a woman of seventy five her skin was remarkably good, clear and very soft; but her movements, unlike those of her neighbour, were slow and quite laboured. She walked with a strange shuffling gait, and a few nasty falls in the past year had made her realise, sadly, that her days of travelling the world, one of her main sources of pleasure, were most probably at an end. Ironic, really, as it now looked as though everyone else's travels were over too!

She looked across at her agitated neighbour and, making a snap decision, struggled out of her chair and puffed,

"Now, Florence, before you go home let's both have a nice big glass of scotch. It'll help us to sleep."

"Oh, Hilda, I couldn't possibly...no, no my dear...I don't usually have anything more than cocoa – which was very nice, by the way – but scotch...oh dear me, no..."

She was still protesting when she stretched out her hand to take the proffered tumbler from her neighbour,

"There you are, dear, you'll enjoy that. Nothing is 'as usual' any more!"

"True…true…" Florence took a large gulp of scotch, "What are we going to do…? What on earth are we all going to do? I can't imagine…"

To deflect Florence from recounting for the third or fourth time that evening all the things she couldn't imagine in the prevailing situation, Hilda cut in quickly,

"Have you seen anything of Maisie, dear?"

"No, nothing at all. I think a couple of women went round yesterday to make sure she was alright, but no…I mean do we really expect to? She'll stay locked in her own little world as always…dear oh dear…"

Maisie Wood, Florence's neighbour on the other side, was a recluse and, apart from those who visited in an official capacity, nobody ever saw anything of her. They had tried being neighbourly but she kept the doors shut and the curtains drawn. The old couple in the fourth house, Mr and Mrs Banyard, occasionally passed the time of day over the garden fence and the fifth house was currently standing empty.

Chapter Eight

"What the hell do you think you're doing?"

Incandescent with rage, Gordon was striding across the field…his field…Claudia's field…the field where she loved to spend her afternoons putting her beautiful show horses through their paces; a field that was now being decimated…dug up…completely ruined by a bunch of oiks with a digger. He waved his stick to get their attention as he was doubtful they could hear him above the racket of the huge yellow machine that was spewing out clods of earth to add to the growing pile just this side of the wall.

Brian Harris signalled to his man to stop the machine, then turned towards Gordon who was now leaning on his stick and trying to get his breath back.

"I said…" he panted, "…What the hell do you think you are doing?"

"We're digging, Gov'nor."

Gordon took three very deep breaths and managed to restrain himself from striking Brian smartly across his back with the stick.

"You are digging on my land and without my permission to do so."

"That's right." Brian confronted his adversary, who was now breathing more normally and awaiting the explanation as calmly as he could.

"You see, last night the lads and me got to thinking that we've been along the wall and we've been up the wall, but, so far, we 'aven't tried to go under the wall. We got well excited by the fact that tunnelling our way out may be the solution to our problem. We did try to phone you at about half past five this morning, Gov. but we was told it was too early to disturb you and the misses, and we didn't want to wait so 'ere we are."

"This is outrageous! You simply cannot do this. You will put back the earth you have moved so far and clear off! There are any number of places you can dig, in fact I don't care where else you dig, but you can't dig here."

"Ah, but you see, Squire, we have to. Cos when we got to thinking and talking we got to looking as well. We found some old maps of our villages and your field here is one of the few places that don't have no cables, pipes and such like running under it. So this field it had to be."

Gordon was beside himself.

"If you and the rest of this crowd don't clear off my land I'll…I'll…"

"You'll what, Sir?"

Brian waited calmly for Gordon to finish the sentence which he failed to do. What exactly was the law in the new order of things? Brian continued,

"I think you'll find, Mr. Golightly, that anything anyone can do to try and sort this out should be done. We're all in it together and the old order don't apply no more."

He turned and signalled once more to the man in the huge machine which began to dig again, immediately and very noisily, while Gordon stormed off across the field, back the way he had come. Many pairs of eyes followed his retreat with some amusement as, in the absence of anything else to do, quite a crowd had gathered to watch the progress made by the digger. This must be the solution; they waited anxiously, biting nails, twisting fingers and pacing back and forward, for the triumphant shout that would surely come: 'we're through!' Everyone wanted to be first to scramble under the wall to the other side and run for help.

By midday, after nearly six hours of solid digging, Brian gave the signal for the machine to be silenced for the last time and turned to face the crowd, shaking his head and spreading his hands in a gesture of despair,

"Sorry, folks, we've gone down as far as we can; it's no use…there ain't no end to it."

A few women started to cry quietly, some leaning on the wall and others clinging to husbands or partners in a mood of helpless, hopeless acceptance. The gang of young people standing or slouching sullenly around Simon suddenly broke and charged towards the wall, picking up clods of earth and flinging them as hard as they could against it, shouting at the tops of their voices. Everyone watched in amazement as the muddy tufts bounced off and fell to the ground leaving no mark at all, not even a speck of dirt where they had touched. Kevin ran forward and kicked at the wall several times before flinging himself down and beating the ground with his fists.

Carolyn and John were not among the spectators at Claudia Golightly's field that morning. In a mood of quiet contemplation Carolyn had set off early, striding down the village street, humming softly to herself with a straw basket swinging at her side as she made her way towards Barry Munden's butcher's shop. She felt strange, but not the sort of strange she thought she ought to feel. It was Tuesday 18th January, exactly a week since the wall had come down – or was it up? Who could say? – and she felt liberated. Yes, that was it. Liberated. She smiled to herself; it was crazy, how could you feel liberated when your liberty was the very thing that had been taken away? She breathed deeply and looked around, savouring the day, mild and damp after some heavy overnight rain. A watery sun sparkled on droplets of moisture trembling in the hedge and threw fingers of light across her path. She and John had listened to the rain in the dead of night, their hands just touching, warm and still after making love. It was a long time since they had made love on a Monday night; what with the pressures of both their careers, they had scarcely ever seemed to arrive in bed at the same time in the last few years. And if they did their talk was usually about problems – wayward children; pompous, unhelpful governors; awkward, over-ambitious parents; insurance claims that may or may not be genuine – they seemed interminable and somehow time for each other had evaporated, got lost, swallowed up in the endless round of family and career related chores.

But last night had been different; it was almost, Carolyn reflected, as though they were starting to rediscover each other. They had laughed and talked about no pressures, after all they couldn't get to work, yet the pressures should have been much greater. They should have been worrying about their very survival, but they weren't.

"It's strange…we all know life is finite, yet we stop making space to enjoy ourselves, thinking I suppose that there will be a golden time up ahead when we can make up for all the lost pleasures, that's if we ever think about it all while we're rushing headlong into each day, like lemmings. But with this wall…well…we really don't know what tomorrow may bring or how long we can survive."

John was murmuring against Carolyn's cheek and stroking her hair as they lay in bed, clinging to each other and she knew he was right. She had pulled a little way away and looked at him, studying the outline of his face in the light from the passageway, the face of the man she loved, and whispered,

"I think I can bear anything if we are together – and with the kids, of course."

He had looked at her without speaking and she was pleased and ready to respond when she had felt the pressure of his hand on her thigh, drawing her towards him.

Afterwards, listening to the rain, they had giggled quietly, relieved to know that water was still falling freely into their strange, new world.

"Whoever would have thought we'd be glad to hear rain?"

Carolyn whispered and John eased himself up, leaning on one elbow,

"I think tomorrow I'll clean out that old water butt, then if our supply does dry up, we'll at least be able to try and collect the rain when it falls."

He was quiet for a moment, then continued,

"I'll go down to the barn as well, see what I can find that might be useful – like Jack said." He sounded quite enthusiastic, then paused before murmuring more thoughtfully,

"That was odd wasn't it…you know, Jack appearing at the meeting the way he did? Did you see where he came from?"

Carolyn thought for a moment,

"No, I didn't, but did you notice, everything seemed to change after he had spoken…people were calmer, somehow."

"Yes, you're right"

John kissed his wife, an unhurried, lingering kiss, before turning over to sleep and Carolyn made her own plans for the next day. She would go to the local shops and see what they'd got left; she would get meat and vegetables and make huge pots of soup and stew. She turned onto her back, flinging an arm above her head, conscious of a feeling of excitement that made sleep impossible. She felt as if she was on the verge of an incredible adventure; it was ridiculous, but the feeling wouldn't go away. It was like a bubble of pure joy growing inside her and she became aware of a smile spreading across her face. It was insane, absolutely insane. Maybe this was what happened to people who were about to die; perhaps this crazy feeling of inane happiness was what made it bearable, but if so why had no-one ever told her?

School…her normal life…seemed a million miles away and she remembered similar feelings of intense joy just after she had married John. She was there again on honeymoon deep in the countryside walking alone on that clear spring day her senses heightened, everything intensified. The sky was impossibly blue, a bluer blue than she had ever remembered seeing before; the air, sharp against her cheeks, had made her laugh out loud and she had flown along the country lane, leaping, bounding and laughing. And that was how she felt now; inside she was leaping, bounding and laughing as she listened to the rain hammering on the roof.

She remembered the joy of cooking meals for her young husband, the care with which she had selected the ingredients from local shops, determined to buy and prepare only the best from the finest produce she could afford. Suddenly she was back again in the delicatessen halfway up the village street, savouring the mixed aromas of coffee, fresh bread, rare cheeses and exotic meats. She remembered waiting her turn while elderly gentlemen ponderously selected their treats from glass fronted cabinets. Cheeses were cut with wires into proper cheese shapes and carefully wrapped in paper that crackled. Coffee beans were put into a machine with a glass funnel and metal tube then, with a noise like gravel in a food processor, had disappeared from the glass, dropping as grounds into a bag strategically placed for that purpose.

Carolyn was brought sharply back from her reverie by the sound of shouting coming from the direction of the small parade of shops where a large crowd had gathered. As she drew nearer, she saw that they were pushing and shoving each other in an attempt to be the first through the doors of the butchers or the small greengrocers a few doors away. Some started to run down the road, towards the mini-mart where the scene was exactly the same. She was actually surprised it had taken this long for people to become desperate and want to stock pile as much food as they could grab from the few shops that remained in the three villages. She felt sure it was only the belief that the wall must be about to disappear overnight as suddenly as it had appeared, that had prevented these ugly scenes from occurring earlier. Most people probably reasoned that, by the time they had emptied their freezers, everything would have returned to normal and they would be stocking up at the supermarkets in town as usual; no need to fall back on the village shops. It had taken a week for this level of panic to set in and, in the absence of the shrink-wrapped goodies they were used to, the local produce suddenly looked tempting enough to fight over.

Carolyn hung back, more than a little intimidated by the waves of aggression emanating from the angry crowd. Fists were waving as people elbowed their way forward, kicking and shouting, furious that they were unable to gain entry as the terrified shop-keepers cowered behind their locked doors. A burly, thick-set man with a bald head and heavily tattooed arms broke free, ran across the road, grabbed a brick and hurled it as hard as he could at the butcher's shop window. The glass should have shattered into a thousand pieces, but it didn't; instead, the brick bounced back, striking a young woman on the head before falling to the ground. She screamed, clutching the place where the brick had hit, but was prevented from falling herself by the mass of bodies seething around her. Carolyn saw the blood spurt from the wound, quickly covering the side of her face and matting her hair. Her eyes were closed and her head was lolling around as she was moved about like a rag doll by a mob of people oblivious to everything except their own perceived needs.

Carolyn took a step forward, determined to try and reach the injured woman, but suddenly, before she could go any further, everything stopped. The shouting voices were quiet, fists uncurled and the moving sea of bodies became still. Turning towards the, miraculously unbroken, butcher's window, Carolyn saw why; Jack was standing with both arms raised, looking around very slowly, his eyes seeming to rest on each person in turn and it was having the effect of making everyone suddenly see exactly what they were doing. It was as if their own eyes, not Jack's, had swivelled inwards and focused on their consciences, as if they were, for a moment glimpsing their own souls. The tension was released and, as people visibly relaxed, they became aware of the injured woman who had slipped slowly to the ground as Carolyn reached her side and caught her just in time to stop her from banging her head on the road. A man took off his jacket and placed it under her wounded head, while Carolyn knelt and took hold of her hand. The woman moaned and her eyelids fluttered as she began to regain consciousness then suddenly Jack was there, helping her to her feet. Carolyn turned towards him to question the wisdom of this – surely she should remain where she was for a little while longer – but was prevented from doubting anything he did the moment she looked into his eyes. She had never seen such calm assurance and a wave of total confidence passed through her. She watched in awe as Jack placed his hand over the injury, quite a deep gash in the side of the woman's head, and the blood slowly disappeared. When telling John all about it later she tried to remember, in answer to his questions, what Jack had in his hand, and decided it must have been a cloth, though she couldn't really remember seeing one. The woman blinked and smiled.

"You'll have to go down the health centre and get that stitched love," a kindly voice shouted from the crowd and Jack turned,

"That won't be necessary. It's not as bad as it looked. You know there's always a lot of blood from head wounds."

Some people were frowning; it did seem a bit odd that she'd recovered so quickly; and one of her friends was examining the place where the brick had hit.

"He's right. There ain't hardly nothing there to see."

Jack smiled at the woman,

"How are you feeling?"

"Fine…yes, thank-you…I feel fine" The woman was gently prodding the spot where the brick had hit her and smiling at Jack with a slightly bewildered expression on her face.

Leaving her with her friends, Jack started to walk back to the front of the crowd, turning for just long enough to smile briefly at Carolyn and thank her. She smiled back and muttered,

"No problem, glad to help," then watched as he stood again between them and the shop window.

"If you all form an orderly queue, Mr. Munden will open his shop…" There were disgruntled mutterings and someone shouted,

"Yeah, mate, and all the meat will go to the ones at the front…"

Jack held up his hand and the man was silenced at once,

"There will be enough meat for everyone, and if you do the same at the green grocer's and the Mini Mart you will also find that you will be able to purchase everything you want. At the moment you all still have money (how did he know that?) so buy just enough to satisfy your needs for today and tomorrow. The shops will be closed tomorrow, but open again the day after – that's Thursday."

The quiet confidence flowing from this man and the authority with which he spoke had the desired effect. Queues formed at each of the shops and everybody bought only what they needed. Carolyn smiled to herself as she saw Jack listening carefully to one old lady who tentatively enquired as to whether she may have two little pots of paste, or should one be enough for both days. She went away beaming as he placed both pots in her basket with a wink and a smile.

John Thompson sat on an upturned box in his barn and made a plan. Like Carolyn, he too felt a ridiculous, totally irrational sense of excitement that he could neither account for nor explain; but as he looked around a dream took shape and grew until he felt compelled to leap up and walk out into the hazy sunshine of that extraordinary January day. He walked down his garden and stared at the unkempt vegetable plot and the patch beyond that he had been meaning to clear for at least the past five years. He could see it so clearly; the vision of what he could achieve here unfolded before him and he was bursting with excitement. He saw rows and rows of well-tended vegetables, pigs snuffling around in the mud and chickens scratching under the fruit trees in the tiny neglected orchard beyond.

He went back to the barn and…yes…there at the back, under a lot of old furniture and other rubbish was the wood-turning equipment he had bought for himself three years ago. He hadn't told Carolyn as he had wanted to surprise her when he completed his first object, but it hadn't even been out of its box. He managed to extricate it and spent half an hour unpacking then setting it up, after which he sat down again on the box and looked at it; he couldn't wait to get started, but first things first. This was about survival – it sounded melodramatic but it was true – so there had to be a coherent plan of action. He had brought a large pad of paper and pen with him to the barn, so he set to and after an hour had drawn up a plan which would turn the dreams into reality. He smiled to himself as he remembered how Carolyn always teased him for his incessant planning, but he knew she secretly approved and was, in fact, very good at planning herself, though not to the extent of computerising everything the way he did. Of course, that method was denied him now, but no matter, he would use the resources available.

Half an hour later, he was still concentrating so hard on fine-tuning the plan that he was unaware of Carolyn as she walked quietly into the barn and crept up behind him. He jumped as she rested her chin on his shoulder and started to study his morning's work.

"Mmmm…I like it. I like it very much."

She broke away from her husband and looked slowly around the old barn. It was huge and she noticed that John's plan so far used very little of the available space.

"What will you do with the rest of it?"

"I don't know yet."

Carolyn smiled at her husband's face and she knew then that he felt the same as she did about their situation. Maybe they were just a bit crazy.

"Come up to the house and have a coffee; I've got things to tell you about my morning."

John listened as she recounted the business at the shops and he looked thoughtful when she came to the part regarding Jack's intervention.

"Why do you think the window didn't break?"

"I don't know, unless Mr. Munden has specially toughened glass – yes that must be it; he's had special glass installed in case of attempted robberies."

Carolyn thought for a moment, then continued,

"But, you know, something else I've only just realised…when Jack was standing in front of the crowd, the first time when he calmed everything down, he looked much taller somehow. He towered above us…yes, that was it…we were looking up at him."

"Probably a sort of illusion, you know because he was commanding attention – a stature thing."

"Yes, that must be it."

Carolyn made sandwiches for lunch which Rebekka ate without a murmur, then announced that she and Kylie were going to walk to the wall. Carolyn managed to hide her surprise; Rebekka and Kylie never walked anywhere, but it was something that people were doing now. The wall was a source of fascination and people were drawn there, mystified as to why no-one ever appeared on the other side of it. Where were all the people who should be missing them? Why weren't there crowds on the other side trying to rescue them? People stood for hours at a time hoping to see relatives who must be wondering where they were, hoping against hope to be the first ones to shout that help was on its way. It was ridiculous; even on a more prosaic level, why weren't employers concerned about the fact that people hadn't turned up for work? And who, Carolyn wondered, was running Bartrum Primary School in her absence? Try as they might, no-one could find any answers to these questions. It was totally baffling.

John got up from the table,

"OK you two, if you've nothing better to do I could do with a hand in the barn. There's loads of clearing to do and a few holes in the roof to mend."

Carolyn waited for James and Jake to protest, but to her surprise they leapt up from the table and followed their dad out of the door,

"Ok, dad, we're up for it."

"Yeah, sounds good."

Left on her own in the kitchen, Carolyn chopped, seared and stirred until two very large pots, one of soup and the other of beef carbonnade, were bubbling on the stove. Sunlight filtered through the window and the grandfather clock ticked steadily on through the afternoon. She couldn't remember the last time she had been able to enjoy cooking food from fresh ingredients without having to worry about some school work she should be doing instead. She had forgotten how satisfying such practical work could be and she felt like an earth mother feeding her family on good things. She loved the woody smell of the parsnips, and the fact that the celery was still covered with black earth which she washed off down the sink, squeezing the little sooty clumps until they crumbled to dust. She wondered why she had allowed herself to be seduced into thinking that having a profession was more important than this.

Suddenly she stopped stirring the soup and stood stock still, her mouth falling open as something struck her. She had been going over again in her mind the extraordinary scene she had witnessed that morning and she realised that Jack had called her by name, 'Thank-you, Carolyn,' That's what he had said…yes that was definitely what he had said, 'Thank-you, Carolyn,' but how on earth did he know her name? She resumed her slow stirring, gazing out of the kitchen window with a puzzled expression on her face, and then concluded that someone must have said it in his hearing. Yes that was it; someone must have said it.

As it started to get dark, John and the boys burst in, cheeks flushed, bringing with them cold draughts of fresh air, sharp and sweet-smelling. Carolyn looked anxiously out of the window, wondering if she should have let Rebekka go as far as the wall; but she needn't have worried. Her daughter came into view through the gathering dusk then appeared in the kitchen moments later trailing her own share of frosty air.

The soup went down well and the boys waited eagerly for their plates to be filled with the main course.

"What is it?" Asked James, wafting the steam towards his nostrils with his hand. Jake did the same.

"Mmmm, smells like booze."

Carolyn laughed,

"It's beef and vegetables cooked in beer. The alcohol tenderises the meat."

"It sure does," muttered James with his mouth full, "this is lovely, Mum."

"It's actually called 'Carbonnade de Boeuf a la Flammande,'" John informed his sons between mouthfuls, "Mum used to make it a lot when we were first married."

He winked at Carolyn.

"Cor, you were lucky," mumbled Jake also enjoying his food, "Why haven't we had this before?"

"Probably something to do with the pressures of running a Primary School and all that entails. Just too damned tired most of the time, but since my efforts are so appreciated, who knows what might appear on the table in future?" Carolyn smiled at the boys, determined to be positive; they all realised the other side of that statement was that no-one knew anything about the future at the moment, where the food would come from and for how long.

Famished after her walk, Rebekka enjoyed a large bowl of soup with some bread then sat gazing hungrily at the dish of Carbonnade. It was several years since she had eaten meat, but she knew it was unreasonable to expect her mother to find different food for her at this difficult time. Carolyn looked at her daughter and said gently,

"Would you like to try some, Rebekka?"

Rebekka glanced at Jake waiting for some sarcastic remarks, but he looked up and said, quite kindly,

"Yeah, go on, Bekks, you can be a Veggie again when the wall goes away."

She smiled at her mum, and Carolyn put a moderate amount on her plate then watched with satisfaction as her daughter finished it all.

Chapter Nine

It was raining on Monday as people from all three villages piled into Gordon's barn for the meeting. They shook wet umbrellas outside the door, then crowded together, sitting on straw bales or anything else they could find. Carolyn noticed that the divisions between the villagers still existed, but were not as marked as before; there was some intermingling.

Once again Gordon had made sure that there was a platform for him and his fellow Chairmen, and David Gibbons groaned as he saw the loud hailer in central position on the table where the three men sat. At nine o'clock precisely Gordon banged a gavel on the table in front of him and stood up, raising the loud hailer to his lips as he did so.

"Thank-you all so much for coming out on this terrible morning…" he began in an oily voice calculated to win people over right from the start; there would be no little interloper stealing his thunder this time. Oh no! He had already looked very carefully around to make sure that Jack was nowhere to be seen. One or two people glanced at each other and rolled their eyes. Did Gordon really think they would be there listening to his drawl if there were any choice.

"He makes it sound like a bloody Charity Auction or something, as though we've all turned up out of the goodness of our hearts. What planet is he on?"

"I don't know, but I wish it wasn't the same one as me!"

Gordon glared over to where David and Ernie were whispering together and they smiled at him.

"Carry on, Gov." Ernie quipped and Gordon looked away, clearing his throat as a flush of anger crept slowly up his neck. Clive Swift and Peter Cunningham were sitting either side of him as before, waiting patiently. Gordon continued,

"Now, ladies and gentlemen, it is obvious to all of us that the situation which precipitated our previous meeting, and which is the cause of considerable angst, still prevails…"

"He means the wall's still 'ere." Said Brian, in a voice loud enough to cause a ripple of amusement around the barn. Gordon ignored him and carried on,

"It seems to me that we must take serious steps to deal with this. We will need committees for everything; my esteemed colleagues…" he paused to smirk, looking first at Clive then at Peter, "…and I will proceed to organise you all into working groups. Each group will have a leader and you will be given different tasks to perform. The leaders will, of course, submit progress reports to us and we will issue further instructions to each group through them…"

"What the hell is he on about," muttered Ernie.

"I don't know, but I think I've just lost the will to live," replied David through gritted teeth. He glanced around at the despondency and drooping shoulders everywhere, then suddenly, out of the corner of his eye, he saw a movement near the platform. And there he was – Jack – standing to one side just like he did before, as though he had materialised out of nowhere. He smiled at the crowd and a cheer went up; there were shouts of,

"Hello, Jack, good to see you…"

"Thought you'd deserted us…"

"Great to have you 'ere, lad…"

Gordon sensed the mood of the crowd and, forcing his face to assume what was supposed to be a smile, he greeted Jack,

"Yes…of course…it's…er…jolly good to see you…and I'm sure that if you heard my proposal for the way forward you will agree that it is the only way…"

Hoping he had gained pole position he paused. Jack smiled,

"Yes…quite. I think, if I may, I would like to ask a few questions."

Jack continued to smile and Gordon, his lips drawn now to a thin line, said nothing but indicated that the floor was his. Jack turned to face the crowd and everyone visibly brightened, straining forward to hear what he had to say.

"I am interested in your thoughts and ideas about how we might deal with the situation; survival is the name of the game and I wondered if, for instance, anyone has found anything that may be useful or perhaps thought of ways in which they might employ their own talents? I am supposing, of course, that the resources we have will remain with us. Let's assume that the water, gas and electricity supplies won't be cut off."

He looked around and waited patiently for someone to begin.

Florence, standing next to Hilda, tentatively raised her hand and Jack nodded in her direction,

"Well…I…er…I went up into my loft to have a look and I found a lot of wool…and needles…and knitting patterns…" Her voice trailed away as she saw Gordon roll his eyes and heave an exasperated sigh. Jack silenced him with a look,

"Please go on, Florence." (How on earth did he know her name?) She continued,

"I just thought that we will need some new, warm clothes and there's nowhere to buy them so some of us could get together and…er… do some knitting."

There were murmurs of agreement and nods from all over the barn as some of the old ladies, who had been doubtful about attending the meeting, convinced that they had nothing to contribute, began to see that they could be useful. Feeling more confident, Florence continued,

"I'm sure Hilda here will help me and we could…"

Hilda gave a snort,

"You go ahead, ducks, and do your knitting; I think there's plenty around here who will help and good luck to you. For meself, I dug out my old dungarees and wellies…I'm hoping to get out in the fresh air and grow stuff. I used to drive a tractor on me dad's farm when I was younger, I could always have another go at that."

There was a burst of laughter at the thought of this feisty, white-haired old lady careering around on a tractor; and the ice was broken. Everyone started talking at once and the noise in the barn rose to a crescendo. Ideas were flowing like water and people moved from group to group, drawing each other in. Introductions were made and plans took shape,

"I've got plenty spare seed that you can have…

"Yes…I'll hatch out some chicks in the spring, then you can have some and in exchange…"

"Come over here, ladies, I know you all like baking bread…what about a bakery? We could open up Cooper's old shop and sell it there…the mill in Lower West Side still works and there are bags of flour stored there, then when the harvest comes in…"

"…And cakes…we could sell cakes too…"

"What about a swap-shop for clothes…?"

And so it went on, people criss-crossing the barn to discuss the possibilities that were growing up around them like mushrooms. The air was buzzing with excitement as hands waved and people leaned towards each other, eager to join in.

Suddenly a loud banging brought everything to an abrupt halt and all eyes turned to where Gordon was beating the gavel down on the table with full force.

"Ladies and gentlemen…PLEASE!!!" He ran his hand through his hair, "your enthusiasm is commendable, but we must have some organisation here! The three of us – he indicated his co-Chairmen again – the three of us will take your names and decide which groups you might possibly be able to join. We will then arrange a time to discuss your proposals…"

People looked baffled; things had been flowing so nicely that all most of them wanted to do was go away and get on with the work they planned to do. Gordon continued,

"Have you, for example, thought about what you will use for money when what is in your purses runs out?"

"Ever heard of bartering, mate?" someone shouted and several voices rose in agreement. Gordon looked flustered and, ignoring him, Jack stepped forward,

"Well done. From what I've heard there are some brilliant ideas and we need to get started. We are now, through no fault of our own, an isolated community; our survival depends on supporting each other and sharing all our resources. If you are greedy or steal you are weakening the group; everyone has a place and will have a job to do; everyone is valued."

Simon and his group of youths shifted uncomfortably. They had no intention of joining in with this bunch of geriatrics with whom, it seemed, they were now incarcerated. But why was the guy out the front looking at them as though he had read their minds?

Gordon tried again, determined not to be upstaged.

"This is all very well and good," he drawled, "but we simply do not have the resources to sustain many of the plans that are being discussed. We cannot, with the best will in the world, produce everything we need; and how can we possibly – realistically – assume that our amenities, will continue…?"

"We can, because we must," Jack cut in firmly. "For as long as we have water, electricity and gas, we will simply go on using them. At the moment the few shops we have are well stocked, so let's keep buying what we need, and when the money runs out, try bartering there too. Money itself is of no value now. There will, inevitably, be problems that arise and need to be solved. Let's meet here at this time every week, a sort of council, and talk through any that have arisen, if that's alright with you, Mr. Golightly."

Gordon gave a curt nod of agreement – what else could he do? And, as everyone started talking again, swapping ideas and arranging to meet, he crept to the back of the platform with Clive and Peter where they stood, an unlikely alliance, whispering and scowling. Jack moved around chatting to people who shook his hand and patted him on the back before leaving the barn in excited groups.

Chapter Ten

Upper West Side, Lower West Side and Middle West Side became hives of bustling activity the like of which had never been seen before. Doors were opened, people talked to neighbours they hadn't previously met, friendships grew, alliances formed and teams were created by like-minded people to perform tasks using skills they had forgotten, or never knew, they possessed.

Notices went up all over the villages informing everyone of what was happening. Cooper's old shop In Middle West Side did open and people queued outside the door every day to barter for delicious crusty loaves and mouth watering cakes produced by the baking group. When they saw how successful this venture was, two more groups formed to provide a similar service in each of the other two villages. Those who were interested in doing so presented themselves to their local farmers ready to perform whatever tasks were necessary in winter to ensure successful crops.

The sheep, pigs and cows also needed tending, and both men and women who were more used to putting on suits in the morning and sitting in offices all day, tramped about in the mud, eagerly responding to the farmer's orders, and looking as though they were loving every minute of it.

Vera, the oldest member of the knitting group at ninety three, declared she had seen nothing like it since the Second World War, and told stories, while they knitted, of families helping each other through those terrible times when you just didn't know where or when the bombs were going to fall next.

"We all pulled together then, you know, just like this…and that was why we won."

And just like the war, everyone was able to cope because in their hearts they believed that the wall, like the war, would, of course, end. They were surviving, doing their bit, and when it ended their lives would be normal again.

At Holly Tree House Carolyn and John set about clearing the overgrown area of weeds and grass at the bottom of their garden in preparation for turning it into a large vegetable plot. It was back breaking work and they were glad that Jake and James seemed only too willing to help. John was surprised, knowing how difficult it was to get them to do their homework, but Carolyn, with her knowledge of young people, understood the difference between that and 'real' work. Watching them, she recalled with a smile the enthusiasm with which the naughtiest children in her classes over the years could be won over by being given real jobs to do. Sweeping up after craft work or tidying the art corner, followed by lavish, and well deserved, praise, sent them home with a glow of enhanced self esteem; they felt useful.

Rebekka disappeared every morning straight after breakfast,

"I'm going round to Kylie's, Mum, and we are being useful – honest – you'll see."

Dumping a huge armful of weeds into the new composter that John had made from bits of wood he had found lying around, Carolyn realised that she wasn't worried about her daughter at all and would be interested to see what she and Kylie were up to, when they were ready to show her. She was, however, very concerned about the number of younger children out playing in the streets because they had no school to go to, and could well imagine the kinds of mischief they would get up to when the novelty of unlimited freedom wore off. The school in Middle West Side that served all three villages was closed as the Head Teacher lived elsewhere and hadn't been there when the wall came down. In fact none of the teachers who worked at the school actually lived in the three villages, but she did wonder while she pulled, tugged and chopped at the stubborn weeds whether there might be any more like her who taught elsewhere and were unable to reach their own schools. And if there were maybe they could....

Her musings were cut short by the sudden appearance of Jack, standing at the edge of the already cleared patch of ground smiling at her.

"Oh," she let out a gasp of surprise and he looked concerned,

"I hope I didn't startle you,"

"No..." She was going to add, 'not at all,' but stopped, and said instead,

"Well...yes, just a bit. But no matter."

It didn't matter, of course it didn't matter, it was insignificant; but she realised that she hadn't been able to lie to this man, even about something so small and unimportant. John and the boys also looked up from their work and Jack greeted them, then turned back to her.

"I hope you don't mind me popping in like this, I can see you're busy doing a great job here, Carolyn, but I wonder if I could speak to you for a moment."

"Yes, of course, I'll make some coffee. Jake, come up to the house in five minutes and you can bring some drinks out here; I'm sure you could all do with a break."

"OK, Mum."

Jack followed her into the kitchen where she busied herself with the kettle and cups. He didn't make small talk, but just sat quietly waiting until after Jake had collected the tray for outside and they were comfortably ensconced by the kitchen fire. There were still plenty of logs left, but she was already thinking about what she could offer the log man in exchange for the next half load.

"Dare I say that you all look as though you're enjoying yourselves out there," Jack began,

"Yes, I think we are. I suppose the whole situation is so weird, and what we're doing so different from what we normally do that it has almost a sort of holiday feel about it..." Carolyn hesitated and smiled a little self consciously, hoping she didn't sound silly. She hadn't really known that was how she felt until she said it.

"Yes, it does, doesn't it? I've been down to Harry Frost's farm this morning and it's great to see all the folk, who are more used to working in the town, feeding pigs and collecting eggs. One of them said it reminded him of the time he spent on a farm as a boy." Jack paused and looked directly at Carolyn before he continued, "I can see that John is going to be in his element developing your land out there, but have you thought about what you will do?"

Carolyn hesitated for a moment,

"Well, help him I suppose. He wants to keep pigs and chickens as well as growing vegetables. And he also wants to work with wood; I don't know how far he'll get with any of it, because it's only until the wall comes down isn't it?"

Jack ignored the question and asked,

"What do you want?"

The directness of the question made Carolyn feel a little flustered, which was perhaps why she answered as honestly as she did.

"I think I should be saying that, like everyone else, I want the wall to go away so that we can all get back to normal, but the truth is…this feels normal…does that sound stupid?"

"Not at all," Jack replied without the slightest flicker of a smile on his face, and she continued,

"It seems normal to spend time together as a family, to cook and eat and talk without all the usual distractions that we've come to accept as normal – clubs, computers, mobile phones, the television, work – it has made me re-assess what normal is."

"Exactly."

She could see that Jack did indeed seem to understand exactly what she meant which gave her the confidence to go on,

"If I was honest I'd say that I want things to go on as they are now, which is absolutely stupid I know because this isn't real…"

"Isn't it?"

"Well no. We're in a bubble aren't we? And trying to survive."

"So, Carolyn, what do you think could be your contribution to the quality of survival in this 'bubble' – for however long it lasts, of course?"

"It's funny you should say that because just as you appeared today I was thinking about the children who aren't able to receive any education at the moment."

"So you miss your career?"

'THE BUBBLE'

Carolyn looked out of the window to where John and the boys were sitting on upturned boxes, drinking their coffee and laughing together at something one of them had said. She turned back to Jack,

"Much to my amazement, no, I don't miss my career at all. I miss the people, my lovely secretary and the children, and I am a little concerned about how they are all coping – it must be such a shock, you know, the fact that I have suddenly disappeared, but none of this is as important as I thought it was. If you had asked me three weeks ago whether I could give up teaching I would have said no. I loved the challenges, the children and the general buzz of my daily life; if I'm honest, I suppose I also rather liked being important, the one to whom everyone had to refer, the one who made the decisions. But at what cost? I was neglecting my family and didn't know it; I was permanently exhausted; everything else except school was marginalised. And all because the job itself, which was once a pleasure, had become impossible, ruined over the last twenty years or so by government intervention. Paper after paper telling us what to do and how to do it, children tested to a ludicrous extent and everyone losing sight of what education is about in the race to try and hit targets. And, of course, the Inspections – what a joke and a bad one at that! Most heads and teachers worth their salt would welcome an objective evaluation of their work by respected professionals, but what do we get? A rag, tag and bobtail group of people who don't know much about teaching and have no idea what to look for! They descend on a school, cause an inordinate amount of stress, then cobble together a report full of inaccuracies, but which is taken seriously by all and sundry because no one challenges the current inspection process. They are worse than useless as they prevent us from doing our work properly. There are many of us trained professionals who know how to do the job, but we're just not allowed to get on with it…I can remember a golden time when we taught creatively, when children were really valued, given time to finish tasks and encouraged to reach their true potential…"

She paused and felt embarrassed,

"Oh, I'm so sorry, Jack, I don't know what made me run on like that…I'll get down off the soap box now"

"It's OK. I asked you a question and I'm very interested in what you are saying. So do you think you could teach like that again?"

"Oh, you never lose it; it's like riding a bicycle, and you do it that way because you know it works."

Jack reached into his pocket and produced a bunch of keys.

"When we have the meeting in Gordon's barn on Monday, I am anticipating that one of the issues brought up will be the problem of the children's education. I happen to know there are three other teachers stranded with us here, but you are the only trained Head Teacher. Will you gather up the children and run the school for us – just while the wall lasts, of course."

"Yes…yes, of course I will…while the wall lasts – and providing my family are happy about it"

He handed her the keys,

"When you've talked to your family, and if they agree, make a list of other people you will need, Secretary, Class Room Assistants, Cleaners and so on, and bring it with you on Monday along with your decision. I've got a feeling there won't be a shortage of people willing to help you. If your answer is no I shall have to think again, but the list will still be useful."

He smiled his most engaging smile and got up to go. Carolyn walked with him towards the door and asked, on impulse,

"Jack, where do you live?"

"Oh…over in Lower West Side…a little cottage. I moved in just before the wall."

Before she could probe any further, the door flew open and Rebekka burst in followed by Kylie. Both girls stared when they saw Jack.

"Hello girls. How's it going?"

"Good,"

"Yeah…good."

Kylie swung her blond hair and gazed at Jack, a winsome little smile playing around her lips. He turned, thanked Carolyn for the coffee and said goodbye then left, waving and shouting his farewells to John and the boys as he went.

'THE BUBBLE'

Chapter eleven

It was nearly six weeks after the wall had arrived that the snow came, huge fat blobs of it, soft and flaky, that fell silently onto the three villages and settled over everything in deep billowing blankets. It was also around this time that people stopped going to the wall.

Although Gordon's efforts to post sentries along there had met with no success, most people were drawn to it, as if by an unseen force, several times a week. They were contributing to the survival of their communities in any way they could, but it was only natural that the real hope for the future should rest in the disintegration of the wall. They would walk there in the afternoons and stare out to where the world beyond was still devoid of any sign of human or animal life. The grass, trees and road continued as before and leaves shivered in the breeze, but nobody ever came near. Some people would arrive at the wall by one road, walk alongside it, perhaps even as far as the next village, then go back home by a different route.

Standing and watching one day, Carolyn was reminded of lions at the zoo, pacing back and forward behind their bars, dreaming, no doubt, of freedom. Then the snow came and the river froze as hard as iron, silvered under a moon which gleamed on the three white villages. It was a magical time with all the joy snow usually brings and none of the anguish; after all they were, to all intents and purposes, already 'snowed in,' cut off behind the wall. They didn't have to worry about tortuous journeys to work or about whether or not the school would open – of course it did, and play times were extended for making snowmen which stood like ghostly sentinels as mothers dragged their children home on sledges in the gathering dusk.

Carolyn had opened the school as Jack asked, and was amazed by how well everything had fallen into place. It was with trembling hands she had unlocked the door for the first time and stood awaiting the arrival of three teachers for a preliminary meeting.

How would they get on? What if they didn't? It was not as if there was any choice; this was not an interview, this was it.

The first one to arrive was a young man and Carolyn smiled, knowing how pleased the mums would be. Try as she might, she couldn't dispel in their minds the idea that a man teacher was a better disciplinarian than a woman, though she knew of many examples which disproved this myth. Dark and quietly spoken, his name was Dan, his strengths Science and Technology and he lived with his wife in Upper West Side. They had no children but, he confided to Carolyn, they had been hoping to start a family very soon,

"...Better put that on hold now, I suppose, until the wall goes; I'm not sure how well the Health Centre would cope with a birth."

He finished with a smile and sat back just as the other two arrived. They were both young, in their third year of teaching and were already friends as they shared a flat together in Lower West Side. Jennie, the quieter of the two, was an infant teacher and an accomplished musician while Maggie, dark and vivacious was more used to teaching juniors and specialised in Dance and Drama.

By the end of an afternoon spent in a discussion so lively and productive that no-one really wanted it to end, the four were ready to welcome children the following day. And, just as Jack had predicted, there had been no shortage of people wanting to help in some way, so the small band of teachers was joined by a school secretary and two cleaners who, like them, were prevented from getting to their own schools. A handy-man called Jed offered to act as Caretaker – "keep the place ticking over for you, like..." and several mums wanted to help in any way they could, particularly with regard to providing a meal for the children at lunch times.

Carolyn was delighted to have so much support and guessed that attendance wouldn't be a problem as the children's unlimited freedom was already beginning to pall with parents struggling to get to grips with a life that didn't involve convenience foods and televisions to quieten their excited offspring.

'THE BUBBLE'

"What shall we do…we're bored," became the all too familiar cry until the school opened. And then the snow came.

There were whoops of delight when Saturday morning arrived and everyone descended on the frozen river, many with their own skates which they found in their lofts or sheds, waiting and waiting for just such a time as this. The air was sharp and cold as people ventured out onto the ice, some gliding confidently at high speed with one hand behind their backs, while others steadied themselves with chairs or clung together laughing and staggering about, trying not to fall.

"..Cor…it must be nigh on twenty years since we've had a winter like this..."

"Yeah…time was we had skating competitions between the villages with silver trophies and all…"

Men in brightly coloured hats and scarves reminisced as they whizzed about the ice, showing off to women and children still trying to find their feet. Shouts and laughter cut through the frosty air and echoed around the nearby gently sloping fields where some families were sliding about on tea trays or home-made toboggans. The infrequency of weather like this meant there were few real, shop bought sledges around, but making do and being creative was already becoming the norm.

Hilda and Florence, huddled in layers of warm clothing, were sitting at one of three available picnic benches sipping hot soup from a thermos flask. With flame-coloured cheeks, they laughed and clapped at the antics on the ice, Florence leaning forward and slapping her hand over her mouth if anyone did anything particularly daring. The sun, bright and surprisingly warm, turned frost covered leaves into jewels, sparkled on the ice and shone on banks of gleaming snow, fast becoming turned, rutted, heaped and moulded by human activity. Huge balls of it were welded together to become snowmen, dads turning into heroes as they managed to lift one onto the other while little ones with hot, red cheeks stared in wonder at the shining results towering above them. All was joy and laughter and no-one wanted the day to end, no-one, that is, except for two who stood back from the rest and watched with varying expressions ranging from disdain to supercilious contempt.

"Oh, see the peasants at play! How very jolly." Gordon surveyed the scene, slapping a short riding crop against his leather boot, while next to him Claudia held a soft, white mohair scarf up to her beautiful, gently flushed cheeks and thought it did indeed look rather jolly. A little further away, Giles O'Dell gazed enviously at the happy, multi-coloured crowd skidding about on the ice and wished he had some skates; he also wished, not for the first time since they had moved to Middle West Side, that he actually knew someone well enough to ask if he could borrow a pair. They hadn't bothered to mix with the local people; Patti said she had absolutely no intention of getting caught up in any of their inane pursuits. She would not be joining clubs or going for coffee to anyone's house and as for the Church….! So Giles had gone along with this, and if they entertained it was their work colleagues and town friends who were invited to the house. He had seen John and Caroline once or twice when Patti had sent him over to fetch Kylie and he thought they looked rather nice; but his suggestion to invite them over for a drink was met with a snort of derision from Patti.

"What, and be treated to an evening of what's happening in the world of education or the even more riveting world of insurance! I don't think so."

His protest that it would be nice to get to know the neighbours…and anyway they may have other interests, was ignored.

Next to him Patti stamped in the snow and shivered, hugging her flimsy little jacket around her,

"For crying out loud let's go! What the hell we're doing standing out here in this filthy snow I do not know. I am frozen."

"You are frozen because you haven't got the sense to put on enough warm clothes," Giles spat back, looking disdainfully at her short skirt and fashionable, but totally inadequate, boots. They would, of course, go, because Patti wanted to, much as he would have preferred to stay and perhaps join in with the fun.

As they turned to leave, Patti felt the unmistakeable sensation on the back of her neck of being stared at. She glanced quickly over her shoulder and found herself looking straight at Gordon Golightly who was appraising her like a prize mare. She tossed her head and looked away immediately, but not before acknowledging that he was, in her book, rather good looking.

'THE BUBBLE'

Chapter Twelve

Mervyn Sculley sat in his study with his head in his hands, reflecting upon the situation, and he had to admit he felt aggrieved. He was tired, bone-weary, just longing for retirement, and now this!

'…Oh God why, at this stage of my career a wall? An invisible wall. A totally incomprehensible, unnatural phenomenon which has wrapped itself around my three parishes when all I prayed for was a quiet removal to the little bungalow that awaits me on the South Coast. Wendy longs for it and I long for it – surely we've done enough…surely! I know…I know the Churches in all three Parishes are practically dead on their feet, but what can I do? You tell me, Lord, because I'm tired of trying to compete with the Sunday morning football and a culture that worships celebrity more than you. I'm sorry but that's how it is…it's not of my making, and I'm tired of the battle. I've had it; and being hemmed in here by a wall is the last thing I needed...'

This despairing mood of self pity was interrupted by a knock at the door and Mervyn looked up as Wendy appeared. Her stooped shoulders and the sad acceptance in her watery grey eyes did nothing to lift his spirits; the only consolation being the knowledge that the reason for her lethargy was not, on this occasion, the result of the demands put upon her by the life of service which she had signed up to on marrying him. She was a perfect reflection of his own state of mind and felt as keenly as he did the unfairness of this unsought entrapment. They had both tried to serve God, initially full of youthful, starry-eyed enthusiasm – they were taking the Gospel out to the masses, they would change the world – and neither was quite sure at what point the struggle became overwhelming and the light had gradually started to go out.

"There's someone here to see you…Jack, I think he's called...oh, and I'm going along to the cottages with some soup for Maisie. She probably won't let me in, but I'll leave it with Hilda; she's about the only one who can make her open the door."

She stepped aside to let the visitor in then left, closing the door quietly behind her.

Mervyn looked at the young man standing before him, the same young man he had watched handling Gordon Golightly so skilfully, and his mood lifted slightly. He smiled.

"Do sit down. What can I do for you?"

"Well, it's rather more a case of what I hope I can do for you."

Mervyn tried to look interested, but he didn't hold out any hope of salvation from this source – unless Jack could make the wall evaporate, of course. He waited and Jack continued,

"It seems to me that your struggle here is an uphill one and you are somewhat battle weary."

Jack spoke sympathetically and Mervyn, whose arms were resting on the desk in front of him, allowed his shoulders to droop and his head to bend as he let out a long sigh. Then he looked up,

"I'm afraid so. Does it show?"

"Just a bit; but you know, I can help if you like."

"If I like…if only it were that simple…" And he didn't really know why, but Mervyn opened his heart to this sympathetic stranger, sharing with him the hopelessness of trying to convince a materialistic society of their need for God, of any sort of spiritual development. He even confessed the guilt he felt at allowing himself to become so discouraged which was, for him, the worse failure of all.

Jack sat very still and listened, never taking his eyes off the weary old man in front of him. When he had finished, Mervyn sat back in his chair and looked a little embarrassed,

"Oh dear, sorry about that…don't know what got into me…shoving all my burdens off onto you like that. Dear me…"

"It's alright," Jack replied with a reassuring smile, "I'm even more sure now that I can help." He leaned forward, "Why don't we begin by stirring everyone up a bit. These are strange times and people may well be more receptive now to the idea that there is a power outside themselves, a benevolent power, a power for living to get them through a situation that is impossible to understand or explain on a purely human level."

"Or they may be more turned off than ever by a God who would allow them to be put in this situation." Added Mervyn pessimistically.

"That's true, but it's a risk we have to take." Jack stood up and walked a few paces away from the desk, then turned again towards the dispirited Vicar slumped in his chair, "come on, Mervyn, let's take some risks," he darted forward and placed both hands squarely on the desk looking straight into the old man's eyes, challenging him, "Do you remember those days, Mervyn? The days when you were on fire for the Lord!"

Mervyn gave a little bark of laughter,

"Ha! Oh yes indeed…we were going to set the world alight. But it didn't happen…it fell on deaf ears and I'm afraid there's only so long that one can go on banging one's head against a brick wall. Only so long that one can care."

"Not true!" Jack spoke with passion, one finger raised in a gesture of authority almost under the startled Parson's nose, "We can energise these people and give them hope, help them to acquire the tools they will need for living in their new world – and we must do it."

Looking back, Mervyn never knew why he hadn't, at that point, politely escorted Jack out of his office and his life, dismissing him as an arrogant upstart, presuming to try and tell him, a trained man with years of experience, how to run his Parishes. But he didn't. Instead they talked all morning and when Wendy returned from a rather trying battle of wills with Maisie, she found, to her amazement, a changed man sitting in her husband's study. He had pages of notes – and plans. Shaking with excitement, he followed her round the kitchen waving large pieces of paper under her nose while she tried to prepare lunch.

"…and we're going to remodel the front of the Church. Look! If we rip out the first three rows of pews we can build a circular raised area for singing and dancing – children mainly – Jack will liaise with the school, he's pretty sure we can get loads more people into Church if we start with the children…involve them, and their parents will come along too. He's also going to speak to Ben who does the football and persuade him not to have practices or matches on a Sunday. After all, if there are no supermarkets or cinemas to visit on a Saturday, it's the ideal day for sport."

He carried on in this vein all through lunch, excitedly shuffling papers and muttering as he absent-mindedly gulped down his soup. At first Wendy regarded him with the amusement of a mother whose excited child has just been picked to captain the school football team. But as she listened she found herself drawn in.

"I can do this because the Church is mine…ours…it belongs to all of us…and I don't have to seek permission from anyone outside the Parish. I can preach as I want without reference to anyone. I can try and reach my parishioners and Jack will help."

The enthusiasm was infectious and she felt something stirring which had been dormant for a long time. At first she didn't recognise it, but as she watched Mervyn hurriedly preparing to go and see Brian Harris about removing the pews, and after she had followed him down the path with gloves and scarf, smiling as she insisted he wear them, she suddenly knew what it was. For the first time in many years she felt the stirrings of hope.

"So you see, Mum, we have been doing something really useful; I told you we were – and we're going to go and see that chap Upwest who does all the posters for everyone and fix a regular day for it."

Mervyn Sculley wasn't the only one bursting with enthusiasm that morning. A very excited Rebekka, pirouetting in front of her mother was, with a lot of arm waving, explaining how she and Kylie had been remodelling clothes using Patti's state of the art sewing machine (which had never been used) in order to start a swap-shop. They had commandeered a small disused building which, many years ago, had been a bank, and were planning to decorate it themselves with tins of purple paint left over from the re-vamping of Kylie's bedroom.

"And we're not just thinking of teenagers, we're going to do stuff for oldies too – and we're going to have a fashion show in the village hall."

Rebekka paused and turned to Kylie, clasping her head in a gesture of exaggerated despair,

"Oh gawd, I've just thought, do we have to ask ghastly Gordon for permission?"

"Maybe we could go and find Jack," responded Kylie, her eyes lighting up, "he seems to be running things now."

"You just tell me when you will be ready and leave that part of it to me," said Carolyn crisply, determined to save Jack from being pestered by a love-struck teenager. Kylie turned to her and said, without much enthusiasm,

"Oh, thanks Mrs. Thompson," then she seemed to appraise Carolyn and, brightening, added,

"Actually, you would be great as a model for the oldies, wouldn't she Bekks?"

Rebekka frowned,

"Do you think so?"

"Yes, she's got a good figure for that age group. Would you do it, Mrs. T? Please."

"Well let's see nearer the time," Carolyn replied, not quite sure whether she should be flattered by the request or insulted by being so firmly and unquestioningly placed in the general category of 'oldie.' She had to admit, though, that she was impressed by the girls' activity. They had produced some lovely outfits from old clothes and seemed to have thought the project through very well.

"What is that racket?" Rebekka asked suddenly, turning and looking out of the window down the garden towards the barn from where the noise was coming. Carolyn made a face,

"It's your brothers…they've started a band."

"Oh stormin'!" Kylie leapt across the room, "Come on Bekks, let's go and see. Maybe we can get them to play at the fashion show. Turn it into a real gig."

And both girls flew out of the door.

"There's several things you all gotta remember, 'cos after that old sow 'as had 'er litter them little 'uns depend on us not getting nothin' wrong. It ain't like the work some of you's used to where a mistake on a bit o' paper can be corrected quick as a flash and no harm done."

There was silence in the barn as Harry Frost looked slowly around the group of unlikely farmers forming a semi-circle in front of him. His eyes rested on Jeremy Golightly and he wondered, not for the first time, just how much longer he would be able to tolerate that arrogant young man on his farm. John Thompson, standing next to him, now there was a different kettle of fish altogether. Sympathetic, sensitive to the animals' needs and quick to learn; you can work with someone like that. And the rest of them were OK; quite a few bankers and other business men who seemed to be loving the outdoor life, riddling potatoes, bagging up the mids and boiling the cracked ones for pig mash. They didn't seem to mind what they did from chitting potatoes to mucking out the sties. It was Harry's opinion that they'd all spent far too long cooped up in offices and lost touch with where their food comes from.

At the end of the line his eyes came to rest on Hilda Bates and he smiled. He'd known Hilda all his life and he was glad to see the old girl looking so well. It was the beginning of March, seven weeks since the wall had cut them off from the outside world, and Hilda was a familiar sight around the farm now. Gone was the shuffling gait as she strode around in her dungarees and wellies, pitchfork in hand, pulling her weight with everyone else. She was pestering him to let her drive a tractor in the spring and, although he'd been pulling her leg, pretending to be horrified by the idea, he was going to let her have a go. After all, his dear wife Mary had done it until her health had failed, so why not Hilda.

'THE BUBBLE'

Everyone listened in respectful silence as Harry continued,

"Now when the old girl's time comes, someone's gotta be with 'er, make sure the placenta comes away right and don't wrap itself around a little 'uns face." he glanced affectionately over to where a large fat sow was lying in a crate, snuffling and fidgeting, as she waited to be free of the piglets stirring inside her.

"We got the lamp there ready to keep them warm and you can all see that the crate is big enough for her to turn in, but not so big that she can roll over and squash 'er piglets."

"How do you know when she's ready to give birth, Harry?" Asked John Thompson softly, reluctant to disturb the air of reverence surrounding the impending event, but eager to learn all he could from this wise farmer. Before Harry could answer, Jeremy Golightly's voice cut through the milky warmth of the dimly lit barn, a jarring sound that disturbed the prevailing tranquillity, and caused the dust motes, which had been twirling lazily in shafts of sunlight, to jangle and dance.

"You can't actually – tell, that is. You just have to watch and when she's ready out they come. I used to chuck swill over the fence to the pigs near my Uncle's restaurant in Henley when I was younger…learnt a lot that way about these mucky creatures."

Jeremy smirked, then stood with his arms folded and looked around smugly as though he had contributed something really valuable to the proceedings. The dust motes settled and there was silence before Harry spoke very slowly and deliberately,

"Well is that a fact." He paused and turned towards the crate, "perhaps you'd all like to foller me and we'll go and 'ave a closer look."

The group reformed around the crate, shuffling so they could all see the star of the show as she lay regarding them with a degree of indifference through half closed eyes. Jeremy rocked back on his heels feeling pleased with himself. It was jolly bad luck being stuck here in this god forsaken village surrounded by some freaky wall. And then Dad saying that, since he was here, he may as well make himself useful by finding out what the peasants were up to on the farm. It was alright for Nigel. Trust him to be on his gap year and far away instead of stuck here with the oldies. Well, he'd show these village idiots that he knew a thing or two; he wasn't Gordon Golightly's son for nothing.

There was a soft click and a sudden streak of sunlight widened to a flood as the barn door opened and a tall, lanky figure stood hovering uncertainly in the entrance, casting a long shadow across the floor. Everyone turned and looked,

"Well, really…" Jeremy recognised the newcomer; suddenly he could feel again, as if it was yesterday, the stinging blows of twigs against his legs as he and his brother were chased by a group of village kids, then the sharp stones on the back of his head and the names "…go on toffs, get back to Mummy and Daddy in your big 'ouse…clear off…" Only Mummy and Daddy were getting a divorce and he and Nigel were sent away to school so that the grown ups could fight it out. His father, the philandering sod, came out of it smelling of roses, married the delicious Claudia and moved to an even bigger house in the village, while his Mum got a flat in Henley. She didn't mind, though, only too pleased to be rid of him. He said in a loud voice,

"I should have thought we had enough in here already…"

Harry ignored him and beckoned Kevin in before he could back away out of the door,

"Come you on in, boy, and stand 'ere along side o' me."

Kevin pulled off his cap and walked forward,

"I just thought I'd…well…like come and 'elp out a bit…with the pigs and that…"

Harry made room for him,

"That's alright, boy, you'm just in time. Now then, young Master Golightly 'ere reckons there ain't no way of telling when a sow is about to farrow, well, we know different, don't we?"

Kevin's face lit up with his idiot grin,

"Oh, that's easy, Mr. Frost. You'll notice they start making a nest like Gertie 'ere 'as, then you just rub 'er belly and run your 'and up 'er teat and if it comes away a bit wet, like, then you know she's getting near 'er time."

Harry smiled, "Go on then, lad, you show us 'ow it's done."

Kevin's idiot grin turned into a beam of delight, his naturally stooped shoulders straightened and he walked forward, throwing his cap down on the straw as he knelt to perform the given task with confidence, gently soothing the sow all the while. Harry knew that he could trust Kevin Bailey, son of Ken Bailey, the best farm hand and pig man he had ever employed. He remembered the goofy little ginger-haired lad who used to shadow his dad all through the holidays, and had been saddened by the stories he had heard about him getting into bad company. Well maybe now there was a chance. He smiled and nodded at Kevin who said, still grinning,

"Yep, I reckon she's about due."

Harry looked across at Jeremy and saw, with some satisfaction, the look of disgust on his face as he watched Kevin hold up a hand to display to the group the milky liquid from the end of the teat.

"So, Master Golightly, that's how it's done," he said, then continued, "and while we're at it we might as well clear up a few other little misapprehensions, so to speak. I was very interested to hear as how you chucked restaurant leavings out as pig swill. Very interested, but I would like to make it clear, here and now, that you won't be doing that on my farm. Dangerous, young sir, very dangerous as such a practice can cause the spread of disease. Also, if I remember rightly, you referred to these animals as 'mucky creatures.'"

Jeremy looked uncomfortable,

"Well, yes…and so they are…everyone knows that," He shifted from one foot to the other and looked around for support which was not forthcoming.

Harry raised an eyebrow and looked at the group,

"Some of you have spent a considerable time cleaning out the sties over these past few weeks, can you tell us all what you've noticed."

There was silence, then John said,

"The pigs seem to do their business up one end of the sty and make their beds at the other,"

"Quite right, Mr. Thompson, so they'm very far from mucky."

Jeremy was starting to squirm, but Harry wasn't ready to let him off the hook yet. He turned again to Kevin,

"Can you tell us what them ol' pigs do in the summer, young man?"

"They waller!" Kevin answered loudly and without hesitation.

"Quite right again. They rootles around in the mud and then they likes to waller and, unlike boys what gets mucky for no good reason, pigs waller to cover theirselves in mud and they cover theirselves in mud to stop theirselves from burning in the sun." He paused, then continued, "Young Kevin 'ere learned what 'e knows by lookin' and doin' and keepin' his mouth tight shut and 'is ears wide open. Seems to me if you do the same you might learn somethin' an all."

The last part of Harry's discourse was delivered directly at Jeremy who, bright red from his neck up to the roots of his hair was staring at the floor while the rest of the group tried to hide their smiles. Encouraged by Harry, Kevin told everyone about the necessity of clipping the toshes, "…they'm tiny little teeth, very sharp, two at the top and two at the bottom…" as soon as the piglets were born to prevent them from nipping the sow and causing her to jump up and possibly trample on them. He was able to get right to the end of the explanation without any interruptions at all.

Chapter Thirteen

Florence and her circle of knitting ladies weren't knitting; they were, instead, sitting out in the sunny cottage garden sharing ideas.

"....then we could see if we can have the old bank building on the days when it isn't being used, and swap all the things we make. After all joining in with Rebekka and Kylie on their days to swap our knitted things has worked well, so why not this?"

There were enthusiastic nods as everyone delved into their baskets, keen to show what they had made. 'Something out of nothing' they had called this session and had all agreed to come up with ideas and examples of how to re-cycle objects that would otherwise be thrown away. The problem of rubbish disposal had been on the agenda of Monday's meeting at the barn, and it was agreed that everything which couldn't be burned had to be re-used.

"Quite right too," Vera had shouted, "We had to do it in the war, why not now?"

The enthusiastic buzz rose to a crescendo and Florence clapped her hands, laughing,

"Now, ladies, one at a time if you please. We shall start with you, Daphne."

Florence hardly recognised herself these days. Was she really leading the group? She had never led anything before in her life, but she was loving it.

Daphne held up the top half of a large, empty, plastic bottle and explained to everyone how it could be used as a cloche for delicate seedlings,

"You see, you just pop it over the little plant and wedge it into the ground; it will act as a protection against slugs and a mini greenhouse. You can keep the lid, on or take it off if you think extra ventilation is needed."

She unscrewed the cap and everyone nodded their approval. A keen gardener, Daphne went on to explain how old C Ds could be hung up to act as bird scarers.

"That's all very well, Daphne, but I haven't got much of a garden to scare birds away from. In fact I haven't really got room to grow anything."

The speaker looked despondent and Daphne rose to the challenge, explaining that she could use hanging baskets, window sills and flower pots to produce strawberries, herbs and tomatoes.

"...And you can convert a window box into a mini greenhouse by bending three or four lengths of wire from old coat hangers into a 'U' shape, place the ends in the soil, then punch small holes in a clear polythene dry cleaning bag and wrap it round the box before putting it back on the window."

"Ooooh, can I go next, Florence, as my idea ties in perfectly with that?" a tiny woman, aptly nick-named Minnie, was waving an egg box and, still smiling, Florence said she was sure no-one would mind. Minnie carefully opened her cardboard egg box and held it up like a magician about to perform a trick,

"These make perfect nurseries for your seeds. You just fill them with compost, plant a few seeds in each section, then when they have sprouted, divide them up and put them in the ground, still in their cells."

"...Yes, and when you're doing that you can protect your knees by making kneepads out of old bits of carpet. Just cut two suitably sized squares, slit a hole in each side and run an old tie, scarf or bit of fabric through the slits to tie behind your knees. They make perfect pads for any kneeling work like weeding or scrubbing....Oh, sorry, Florence, it's not my turn."

The speaker sat back looking embarrassed and everyone laughed, then the person sitting next to Daphne described how to make a bird feeder from a coffee tin or, by covering the outside with glue and winding string round it, a useful container could be produced.

And so it continued all afternoon. Ideas flowed like water and the merits of such things as socks for polishing mitts, aprons fashioned out of old shower curtains and used tea bags added to the soil in plant pots to provide extra nutrients were seriously debated.

"And, of course, tea does make an effective polish for mirrors," declared Florence, before producing her 'piece de resistance' – a cushion made from an old sweater and stuffed with plastic bags.

Everyone declared the afternoon a great success and they looked forward to being able to share their ideas more widely, determined to come up with even more ways of making use of everything they could find.

Daphne and Minnie walked home together, warmed by the late afternoon sun, and were discussing some of the ideas they had heard. Suddenly Daphne stopped and looked around her,

"That's what we should be doing! We should be using all this space for growing food." She grasped Minnie's arm,

"Do you remember, about ten years ago a few towns started to use public areas for growing vegetables instead of flowers, and it worked really well?"

"Yes, I remember that…"

"Well, it's obvious, isn't it? We're trying to survive and we need food. Let's take it to the meeting next Monday and see if we can get everyone motivated, not just to grow in their gardens, but out in the public places too. We'll see what Jack thinks…"

"Jack thinks it's a very good idea."

Both women jumped as Jack fell in step beside them,

"Sorry if I startled you, but I couldn't help overhearing and, yes, I think it's a great idea and it will definitely go on the agenda for next Monday.

The green garden gate shut with a soft click as Carolyn made her way up the path to the door, painted in the same gentle shade of green, and knocked. She took in the immaculate garden and watched chickens, bathed in dappled pools of light, pecking and scratching on the bare patch of ground beyond. The sun rippled their feathers in streams of shining russet shot through with gold as heads bobbed, eyes glinted and red combs wobbled. She closed her eyes and lifted her face to the warmth, drinking in the song of the birds in the nearby orchard and enjoying the gentle breeze against her cheek. So absorbed was she in the beauty of this perfect spring day at the beginning of May that she was unaware of the door opening. Martha coughed and Carolyn turned with a spluttered apology, feeling rather foolish.

"What can I do for you?"

Martha's voice was gentle and her smile welcoming,

"Well…I was wondering…that is, I had heard that you are able to provide medicines…cures for ailments made from natural remedies, so I thought…"Carolyn's voice tailed off as she realised she was not making herself at all clear and really had no right to be intruding on the old woman in this way. In fact she wouldn't have come at all except that John's elbow was swelling horribly and the medical centre had run out of anything that could help him. It was just by chance that one of the mums had told her how Martha had given her a tonic which had cured her daughter's cough, so she thought it was worth a try.

"You'd better come in."

The old lady stepped aside and Carolyn found herself in a tiny entrance area illuminated by light flooding into it through an archway directly ahead; she followed Martha into the room beyond and couldn't believe her eyes. It was a kitchen, but unlike any she had ever seen before as, amongst the usual paraphernalia of everyday living, was equipment that looked as though it belonged in a Science Laboratory. There were glass phials, jars and bottles, basins and test tubes all stored neatly on one of the surfaces. The whole length of the longest wall was occupied by a dresser stacked with gleaming storage jars containing what looked like dried flowers and grasses, and decorated on the outside with hand painted flowers. Everywhere was spotlessly clean, neat and tidy, as was Martha herself. Her grey hair was combed into a shining bob and she wore a white ruffled blouse with a grey cardigan and skirt.

"Please sit down," Martha paused, then smiled at Carolyn's expression of disbelief,

"You look surprised. No doubt you thought poor old 'Mad Martha' would be living in squalor."

"Oh no, not at all!" Carolyn exclaimed, colouring, because she realised, even as she protested, that it was exactly what she had been thinking. She also knew that Martha had seen right through her.

"I'm so sorry…it's just that…"

"It's alright. Tell me why you've come."

Martha and Carolyn both sat down at the well scrubbed table and Carolyn told her about John's elbow swelling after he had been sawing wood.

"I think he's got bursitis but the pharmacy down at the Health Centre has run out of the appropriate cream. I wondered if you have anything."

Martha stood up and walked over to the dresser; she opened a drawer, took something out and returned to the table where she placed a small pot in front of Carolyn.

"Rub that on three times a day and the swelling will be gone in under a week."

Carolyn picked up the pot and turned it over in her hands. It was plastic and unmarked apart from a flower fastened securely on the top with the letter 'C' written underneath. Before she could ask the question Martha supplied the answer,

"It's Comfrey Cream, made from a fast growing, tall perennial herb called Comfrey, or Symphytum Officinale, that contains allantoin. Don't worry, it works."

Carolyn smiled at Martha, and in that moment had no doubt that the cream would work and would do John no harm at all.

She looked around the kitchen again, particularly at the array of mysterious jars on the dresser, and suddenly had an idea.

"Would you teach us all how to use natural ingredients as medicines? I hope you don't mind me asking, it's just that we are living in such a strange time and need to help each other in any way we can."

And that was how it began. 'Mad Martha' became the village Apothecary sharing her knowledge and skills with people who would previously have dismissed her as an oddity and not given her the time of day, let alone take her seriously.

The continued supply of gas, electricity and water into the three villages remained a mystery. No bills were paid, of course, as none were received and no-one had any money anyway, but it wasn't long before these amenities were just used and taken for granted. As was the supply of fresh meat and milk. Harry had thought that his few pigs would be fought over to be slaughtered and used for food, but it didn't happen, which was just as well as his old boar had died, heart attack the vet said. It was Hilda who had found him and told Harry who thought at first he was just asleep,

"'That ol' boar's dead,' she said, no, I said, he'm just sleepin,' but I went over 'n' kicked 'im and sure enough the ol' boar were dead,"

The locals at The Rose and Crown laughed when Harry told the story, but the laughter was tinged with nervousness as they still wondered if, or when, the supply of meat would run out. Soon, however, everyone realised that certain foods were, incomprehensibly, in constant supply – as was the beer at the pub, supplied by the locals. It hadn't taken long for the men to start making their own, and producing the best brew provided healthy competition among them. The necessary contraptions and equipment replaced the now redundant cars in many garages. There was no petrol and, as their world consisted of little more than fifteen square miles, people walked everywhere. Ernie Briggs repaired machinery instead of cars and even had an apprentice working with him as Simon, like Kevin with the pigs, discovered he could be useful in this new world, and that it was more fun creating than destroying.

Barry Munden stared at the sides of beef, legs of lamb and hams hanging on great iron hooks from the ceiling.

"It's like that story, you know, when we were kids, about the magic porridge pot that keeps filling up," he told all and sundry when they questioned his source of the best meat they had ever tasted. And he had no answer other than that. All he knew was that every morning when he went into his massive refrigerator the meat he had used the day before had been replenished. It was the same story at the Mini Mart. In fact the only things that weren't supplied were the things they could make for themselves. The baking group continued to turn out delicious loaves, making use of sterilised plant pots and empty coffee tins to add a variety of shapes to the finished products. They also added flavour by chopping in garlic, herbs and onions, now growing in plenty all over the villages along with many other crops.

Chapter Fourteen

22nd July 2020

The Church was full, even the gallery and balcony were bursting with people craning forward to watch the children dance; and when they had finished, rapturous applause rang round the rafters. As it died, Mervyn stepped forward and, looking slowly round at the congregation, clasped his hands in front of him before addressing them,

"That was a real treat, and I can tell from your response that you all enjoyed it as much as I did." There were nods and murmurs of agreement, then he continued,

"Now we have another one for you as Jack will be speaking to us today." Jack rose from one of the front pews and, as he walked forward, there was another burst of applause. Mervyn smiled and watched as the young man ascended the pulpit steps and was amazed at himself. He knew in his heart of hearts that the old Mervyn would have experienced just the merest twinge of jealousy. His sermons were improving, there was no doubt about that, but he never received the same rapturous welcome as Jack. It didn't matter, though, he was learning and the important thing was that the word of God was being heard, listened to and acted upon.

Jack looked round with a dazzling smile and Kylie, sitting between Rebekka and Carolyn, let out a long sigh. Everyone listened with rapt attention as he spoke about God's Grace being sufficient and his power made perfect in weakness.

"You are all new creations, the old has gone, the new has come and God is providing. He is there in even the tiniest details of your lives. You have no money, yet do any of you lack anything?"

He leaned forward and continued quietly,

"Do some of you perhaps feel that the floodgates of Heaven have been opened and so many blessings poured out that you scarcely have room for them?"

There were murmurs in the congregation for, much to their surprise, that was exactly how they did feel. They didn't really know why they had started going to Church again after years, sometimes entire lifetimes, of ignoring or denying the existence of God. Maybe it was fear, unacknowledged but profound, the fear of the unknown, the unfamiliar situation making them feel the need, as never before, of a Divine Presence. Like in the old days before the wall when there was a disaster and everyone started praying and going to Church. Or when a baby was born and the family had it christened without really knowing why as they had no interest in Church the rest of the time and didn't really intend to give any serious thought to the promises they were making.

Something or someone had decreed that a wall should imprison them and yet they were unharmed. They were searching for answers and Church was proving as good a place as any to try and find them. Jack's sermons were riveting, powerful and uplifting; they brought hope and comfort to all who heard them and gradually the Churches in all three villages had become full to bursting. Coaxed in by others, even the most unlikely and reluctant worshippers had ventured over the threshold then returned again week after week, encouraged by what they had heard. The stresses and strains of their old lives had gone; they were content, creative and discovering talents they never knew they possessed. Their world had become small, but many wondered why they had wasted so much time at airports, racing around chasing after...what? And missing the joys that were on their own doorstep.

Jack grasped the sides of the pulpit,

"The tyranny of monotony has been broken for there is a stimulus in Christ that puts a sparkle into life and makes it creative amid the uncreative. We are builders not destroyers, sharing our talents with each other. Most of you are discovering your true selves, you are progressing steadily towards the people you were always meant to be. The guidance is there if only we will listen. When you cling to material possessions the sunshine goes out of your souls; there are so many riches and blessings that cannot be bought with money."

There were nods of agreement from people who, before the wall, would have snorted with derision at such an idea and dismissed Jack as an idealistic nutter. His voice rose to a crescendo as he concluded:

"We are meant to live life with great joy, not worrying about tomorrow, not fettered by fear, not living on a diet of fingernails, but on faith. Let us live joyously, effectively and abundantly today, not concerned about what lies dimly at a distance, but doing to the best of our ability what lies clearly at hand. Let's empty our hands today to receive the gift of peace, then open them again to share that peace with those around us." He paused and raised his arms,

"And may the God of hope fill us with all joy and peace as we trust in him, so that we may overflow with hope, joy and abundant life by the power of the Holy Spirit."

There was another round of applause as he smiled then stepped down from the pulpit, and people left the Church uplifted by what they had heard. They believed Jack as, at the moment, he was all they had.

Carolyn and John walked home from Church in the July sunshine. It had been raining in the night and now everything sparkled. James raced past them, followed closely by Jake

"We're going to pick up our swimming things and go down to the river pool; see you there," Jake shouted as he ran to catch up with his brother.

"Yes...I'll bring you some lunch," Carolyn replied and watched them go. She smiled and shook her head as she thought about the river pool – yet another strange phenomenon in this weird world. It was four weeks ago now since Jake had come home spluttering and gabbling about the water in the river running clear,

"Honestly...you must all come and see...it's unbelievable...it's like a fantastic swimming pool you know where it opens out on the corner near Harry's orchard."

And it was. There were other places too where the river widened near Upwest and Downwest that could also be used as pools, and the really good swimmers were having fun racing between them.

Carolyn boiled the eggs she had collected from their chickens earlier in the day and made salad using lettuce, beetroot, cucumber and tomatoes from their garden. The dirt fell easily from the lettuce root which she then chopped off and put with the coarse outer leaves in the composter ready to take down the garden later. The water ran cold and clear over the remaining leaves, glistening and crisp in her fingers. She looked out at the vegetable patch admiring the neat orderly rows of carrots, onions and potatoes, then her attention was caught by the sun shining on the barn roof.

She smiled as she thought about John and the work he was doing now. It had all started when the March winds had blown down some trees and wrecked a fence in Upwest. David Gibbons offered to remove the trees, but didn't really know what to do with them and no-one knew how to mend the fence. John had stepped in, offered to help and instructed David to drag the wood along to Holly Tree House. He shared his ideas with James and Jake who became as enthusiastic as he was about using wedges to split the wood apart following its natural curves and using this to make all manner of things. The fence was mended and there followed requests for gates and other furniture made in the same individual style. The Thompson family were only too pleased to oblige and everyone was impressed with the results, quirky but sturdy and effective. They were able to reclaim wood from other trees that had blown down and people even started to bring them scrap materials, rusty hinges and other iron work to use that would otherwise be thrown away. Carolyn had never seen John happier than he was now, and the boys both agreed that the new life beat school any time.

The village school was another success story. The team worked well together, so well that when Carolyn had put forward the radical idea that the children should only be taught the skills and talents that would be of use to them in the future, Jenny, Maggie and Dan knew exactly what she meant and were whole-heartedly behind her.

"They need to know how to survive." She said, "Then, on top of that let's work out what else is essential and how best to teach them."

"Tools for living! That's what they need."

Maggie's response was, as always, enthusiastic and the other two soon joined in. Dan's Science lessons were fun, hands on and relevant to their lives. Jenny made sure they could all read and write to the best of their ability and taught them how to have fun with music. They learned to paint as it was agreed that making their surroundings aesthetically pleasing was important. They were taught basic Mathematics and, through Drama, Maggie made them aware of some aspects of History before the wall.

"They have to be developed emotionally, spiritually, aesthetically and physically as well as intellectually," Dan said and they all agreed.

Carolyn was good at helping the children to develop a sense of right and wrong; Jack assisted with their spiritual growth and his thought provoking sessions were eagerly anticipated by children of all ages. They went running round the fields with Dan, played football, netball, rounders and cricket and, since the clear water had appeared, were able to go swimming as well.

But, most of all the children loved making things, and it was this that had given Carolyn her best idea so far. She knew that above all they needed to know where they would fit into this world behind the wall. There was no need for bankers or secretaries any more; many of the professions in the old world were redundant,

"So let's use the apprentice system and the children can learn from the adults who are contributing to the community,"

And this was how Barry Munden, Brian Harris, Ernie Briggs, Harry at the farm and the ladies at the bakeries found themselves with extra help. The school opened for three days a week and for the other two the children aged eight and above were helping all around the villages. They learned to be butchers, shop keepers, builders and gardeners, to look after chickens and pigs, to mend clothes, bake bread and make things out of wood.

'THE BUBBLE'

Convincing the others in the villages that this would work had not been easy, and Carolyn could still recall the shocked expressions on people's faces when she had put the idea forward at one of the Monday meetings,

"Well I can't see me getting me work done with a parcel o' kids running about the place and that's a fact," Brian Harris had said, sourly, and David Gibbons agreed,

"Apart from anything else it's dangerous. I can't work with me tools if I'm baby sitting; and if they muck about what are we supposed to do?"

"I shall give 'em a good clout," retorted Brian, "And no doubt that'll get me wrong with their parents – no it aint gonna work."

Carolyn had assured them that there would only be two or three children at each place at any one time, there would be a mum there to watch them and if there was any mucking about they were to be sent home and she would deal with the culprits on the next school day.

"I think we should give it a try," Jack had said. So they did, and the sceptics had to admit that, to their amazement, it worked. The children responded well to doing 'real work,' and were happy to share their experiences with their classmates and write up their notes on school days. Carolyn had two week days to do the things she wanted to do, the quality of family life was better than ever and her new life, unlike her old, was manageable.

By the time Carolyn was ready to set off and join the others at the river pool, John had already gone, taking with him the heaviest of the two picnic baskets; the boys had asked him to get there early to help make a rope swing that would drop them from a nearby tree into the cold, clear water, and he had said he'd see what he could do. Closing the door behind her – nobody bothered to lock them any more – Carolyn swung down the street, past the little parade of shops and on towards the turning that would take her through Harry's orchard to the river pool.

'THE BUBBLE'

On her way she marvelled at the cottage gardens with their array of flowers and vegetables. She breathed in the scent of sweet peas clinging to the criss-cross of sticks, their pastel shades of papery flowers flickering gently in the breeze like butterfly wings. Runner beans had also climbed high, their berry bright flowers almost ready to give way to tiny green beans that would cling to their stalks like legless caterpillars, hard and shiny. There were sunflowers, full blown and generous, planted against shed walls where they stood guard over vegetable patches: crinkled lettuces, courgettes hidden by pale green foliage and lemony flowers, and dark green spinach leaves. There was a tangle of peas next to well-spaced onions, their green, spiky tops bent over at odd angles, ferny carrots, with orange roots just visible, urging their way up into the sunshine, and earthed up mounds of potatoes, all in neat rows. Honeysuckle trailed around cottage doors sometimes entwined with full, blowsy roses, their scents combining to produce an almost overpowering sweetness.

The weather had been hot and sunny for days but the rain of the previous night had freshened the gardens giving everything an added sparkle. It was perfect, Carolyn thought as she turned down the path towards the orchard. She could already see the river, a glistening ribbon in the distance, and her attention was caught by cricketers in a nearby field, preferring their traditional sport to the novelty of the river pool. She knew that Morris Dancers would be going to all three pubs that evening and was glad it looked as though the weather would hold for them.

The apple blossom had gone and the leaves shivering in the breeze looked bright and healthy; there would be a good harvest of red and green apples, clustered around the boughs, pulling them almost to the ground. Carolyn smiled as she saw the brightly coloured gypsy caravan nestling under the trees. Harry had put it there for the children to use as a play house and she had been told many a tale of the fun they had had in it. On the other side of the path ash keys and sycamore wings trembled on branches, and little tight acorns hung in pairs from a mighty oak that grew just before the path opened onto fields leading down to the river.

'THE BUBBLE'

On one side of the path the corn was golden and ready to cut, while the field on the other bore stubbly remains of hay that had already been safely gathered ready for winter feeding. Hilda, a floppy hat protecting her head, had fulfilled her wish and driven the tractor, bouncing along with a smile on her face from early morning till nightfall had forced her to stop, hoping for good weather the following day.

Carolyn stood for a moment, lifting her face to the sun, and was suddenly aware of the smell of charcoal mingled with the sweetness of warm summer grasses. She knew what that meant; Brian and Ernie had taken their giant home-made barbecue, fashioned out of an old oil drum, down to the river pool and there would be meat a-plenty to supplement everyone's salad, bread and potatoes. Splashes and squeals floated on the distant air, and somewhere overhead, unseen as always unless you had followed its path upwards with your eye, a skylark hovered, its pure, clear notes piercing a sky that was the most perfect blue.

And it was in that moment that she felt suspended; just for that moment everything seemed to stop. Each tiny sound, everything from the song of the birds, the crack of leather on willow, the shouts, the scent of warm summer grass and the bright, glowing scene around her was held in the notes falling one by one from the throat of that unseen bird. Something had happened. Had the world stopped turning? Had the wall gone? Carolyn shook herself, but the perfection of the day was spoiled; a day that had been, perhaps, too perfect? Was it still a fact in this new world that if something seemed too good to be true, then it probably was? Disturbed by thoughts she didn't want to entertain she walked on, quickening her pace, eager to reach the safety of the company of others…her reality.

She enjoyed the afternoon, the cool of the water, the food, the fun and the laughter, but something wasn't right. She was still troubled by that feeling, like she used to get in the old days when she'd forgotten to do something important and couldn't remember what it was. Something had jerked out of place, become dislocated, but what could it be? There was nothing wrong, apart from the weirdness of a life they had all come to terms with now.

Later she did what scarcely anyone bothered to do any more and went to the wall. It was still there, still exactly the same. She walked back to the village and joined John at the pub clapping along with the music, tapping her feet as the Morris Men jingled and stamped out their dances, but still it wouldn't go, the strange feeling that something was wrong; something had changed and not for the better.

'THE BUBBLE'

Chapter Fifteen

"I think we should kill him."

At precisely the moment when Carolyn had stood listening to the skylark on her way to the river pool, Gordon Golightly was uttering these six words. He then sat back and blew smoke from a tiny cigar slowly out from between his lips, keeping his eyes fixed on the two people with whom he was, reluctantly, sharing his space in the shade of his trees next to his large, blue marble swimming pool. Not for him the frolicking with peasants on muddy river banks, however clear the water.

They couldn't be called companions, as there was nothing remotely companionable between him, Clive Simpson and Peter Cunningham. He still despised them and they still feared, and occasionally loathed, him. But they hung together, outsiders, misfits, who couldn't find a place in the new world, drawn together by a common hatred of Jack and all he stood for. They had, all three, been displaced and they didn't like it. Their wives had changed towards them; Norma Simpson, never before known to be anything other than agreeable to the point of subservience, now disregarded Clive's wishes and did pretty well as she pleased.

Marion Cunningham actually had the audacity to hold meetings in the house, filling the place with excited, chattering women, and when she wasn't doing that she was at the bakery. Oh yes, she was happy to make bread for the masses while Peter was reduced to getting his own dinner, something he would never have tolerated in the past. Both women had supported their husbands before the wall, boasting about their elevation to Chairmen of their respective Councils, even using this to lord it over the other women. But now that had all changed, their wives had found friends in the new world and both men felt barely tolerated in their own homes.

Gordon was frequently irritated by Claudia these days. The fact that she was one of the sweetest, loveliest people he had ever met had served his purpose well when he had first married her. She was malleable; she loved him and he could do pretty much what he liked, knowing that Claudia saw only the good in everyone and everything. She would never suspect him of shady deals, risky investments that were not strictly within the law, or marital infidelity. If she had ever got wind of some of the things he was up to he knew he could talk her round. She would have believed him.

Satisfying her in bed was easy and he had to admit that her spontaneous joy did give him pleasure; it was almost a shame really that he still needed the thrill of the chase; still had to know that he could conquer feisty mares like that Gibbons woman or the tarty blond he had seen standing in the snow and who he was now reeling in quite nicely. It was a shame because the pleasure with them was raw and fleeting. It was, at the end of the day, only satisfying his lust – and mainly a lust for power more than anything else. The sex was disappointing; and it was just sex. He had to admit, reluctantly, because to do so meant relinquishing some control, that he loved Claudia. And it was true; inasmuch as Gordon Golightly could love anyone or anything outside himself, he loved Claudia.

She was not at all like Cecilia, his first wife, mother of his two boys and all round pain in the arse. It irritated him just to think of her with her endless questions and habit of standing up to him if she thought he was wrong. Huh! Difficult to be a man in your own house saddled with a woman like that! He was well rid of her. But now Claudia seemed to be getting some really weird ideas. She was helping around the village, lending this, giving that and becoming enthusiastically involved with what was going on. She had even started teaching some of the village kids to ride, and he was sick of the sight of them squawking around the place, bouncing about like sacks of potatoes on the ponies they had bought for Nigel and Jeremy.

And she liked Jack; she enjoyed going to Church and Gordon had to sit at the lunch table on Sundays listening to her recounting Jack's sermons with shining eyes, her voice full of something amounting almost to hero-worship.

"Honestly, darling, I do wish you would come. You would love it; we all do. He makes so much sense and we come away feeling much better about ourselves and everything."

Damn the man! It was almost as if she was being unfaithful, something he knew she would never do, but the jealousy Gordon felt could not have stabbed more severely if that were the case. He hated Jack.

"Kill him?"

Clive fidgeted nervously and puffed out a long breath of air as though he had been punched in the stomach.

"Huh, seems a bit radical, mate!"

Peter leaned forward, rubbing his hands together with an expression on his face that hovered somewhere between a smile of disbelief – Gordon couldn't mean it – and enough interest to intimate that he wouldn't mind knowing more. Gordon drew hard on his miniature cigar and exhaled again very slowly, fighting the urge to tell Cunningham, in no uncertain terms, that he was not 'his mate.' He thought carefully about what to say next; Cunningham, he could see, would be easier to convince than Simpson, little ferret of a man, frightened of his own shadow. It was difficult to say whom he disliked the most, but needs must…be pleasant, they're all you've got. Weighing his words with great care he said,

"Think about it. Do any of us know where he lives? Has he any family, anyone who will notice if he disappears? Oh yes, I know he's got the whole population of three villages eating out of his hand, but he always seems to spring from nowhere. If he vanished people would think he had just gone back to where he came from, wherever that may be. They would miss him…be confused and upset and that's where we would step in. We could emphasise the fact that he was obviously unreliable – full of fancy ideas, but not prepared to stay and follow them through' then we could lead everyone back to our ways, get things organised the way we like."

The other two were listening with interest, Clive all the while taking little nibbling sips of Gordon's brandy (not the best he could offer, of course, but a sacrifice worth making to get his own way) and Peter swilling it round and quaffing it in an attempt to give the impression that he was used to the finer things of life instead of his customary brown ale. They were united in their hatred of the common enemy, completely forgetting that the three of them had never, in the past, agreed on the way things should be.

"It's got to look like an accident, of course," Gordon continued.

"Yes, of course," Peter murmured, nodding and waiting for him to go on.

"What…what sort of an accident might that be?" Clive asked tentatively, taking another little sip of brandy then coughing violently.

"Not quite sure of the details yet…had to make certain you were both on board, you know."

Gordon gave them what he hoped was his most winning smile and wondered how he was going to resist the growing urge to slap Clive – not too hard, just enough to knock him off his chair. Did the silly little man expect him to do all the thinking? He leaned forward,

"And you are, aren't you…both on board, I mean? You can see it's the only way." He looked from one to the other and waited. Peter Cunningham spoke first,

"Well, Gov'nor, I think you may be right. And, as you say, who's gonna miss 'im, eh?"

Clive was silent, still dabbing at his mouth with a white handkerchief following the coughing fit. The other two looked at him,

"Well…yes…I suppose so… as long as it looks like an accident…shouldn't want Norma to find out what I'm up to…"

He turned a shade paler at the thought then, giving a nervous little laugh, took off his spectacles and polished them before returning them carefully to his nose and tucking the handkerchief back into his pocket.

"Right then, what next?" Peter looked expectantly towards Gordon as though he, too, thought he could pull something out of a hat.

"We watch and wait. Try and get some ideas and meet again very soon."

'...but not too soon,' he finished silently as he watched them go, Peter striding out, with Clive picking his way across the lawn next to him and looking for all the world, Gordon thought, as though he wanted to apologise to the grass for walking on it.

Gordon finished his brandy and closed his eyes. When reflecting on what happened next, he could never be sure whether he had slept for a while and then woken, or whether Jack's appearance followed immediately after the departure of the other two men. Either way he was suddenly there, standing in front of him, just watching and smiling; Gordon sat bolt upright, almost falling sideways out of his chair; Jack didn't move and Gordon tried to compose himself. He couldn't have heard, surely; he felt his face reddening at the thought, but where the hell had he sprung from? He cleared his throat and said, in what he felt sure was a normal voice,

"Oh...Hello there! What can I do for you?"

But his feeling of discomfort persisted; once again Jack had wrong-footed him – damn and blast the man. How was he to deal with someone he had been plotting to kill? And why didn't he say something instead of just standing there? He indicated the chair recently vacated by Peter Cunningham,

"Why don't you sit down?"

So Jack sat, relaxing back in the chair comfortably and crossing his legs, but all the while keeping his eyes fixed on Gordon who was, in turn, studying the fresh, young face before him; handsome, fair skin framed by soft brown curls and those piercing blue eyes, clear, dazzlingly bright. Making a snap decision, Gordon leaned forward and spoke softly,

"What's the secret? What do we have to do to get rid of the wall and get our lives back? If you tell me I will give you anything you want"

"You have lives; lives that are richer now than they have ever been. People are happy…contented. Why can't you be happy too, Gordon? You have all this," he indicated their immediate surroundings, rolling lawns, the clear blue water of the swimming pool and the mansion in the distance illuminated by the late afternoon sun.

"You have a beautiful wife; you could, if you wanted, contribute to the life of the three villages. Come to Church; get to know the people around you better, share what you have. What would be so awful about that? What more do you want?" He paused for a moment then added, "I want nothing from you."

Jack also spoke softly and Gordon was enraged. He leapt to his feet,

"A life…I have a life!? This is not what I call a life…paddling about here in the mud with a bunch of village yokels, not able to get away anywhere…my stocks of malt whiskey, the finest brandy money can buy and my special cigars all running low, and you call this a life! What have you done to us you little bastard? You may have brainwashed the others but you haven't brainwashed me – and no I'm not coming to Church to listen to your mealy mouthed drivel, you little shit! You've come here from heaven knows where with your soft talk and you've made them all think they're happy living here behind the wall. Well they're not and I'm going to show them they're not. You think you're so important…you've taken control…you've made me nothing. Well let me tell you…I'm getting it back. I'M GETTING MY POWER BACK!"

Beside himself with rage by now, Gordon was striding about and waving his arms. Out of the corner of his eye he saw a spade leaning against a nearby tree and lunged towards it. What the hell. It may not look like an accident but he'd get the bastard now, smash his head in and bury him deep, then we'll see who's running things. He swung the spade round with great force, but all he hit was the empty space where a few moments before Jack had been sitting.

'THE BUBBLE'

Chapter Sixteen

Nobody knew – how could they? – No-one had any idea that when the spade flew through the air, wooden handle clutched firmly in Gordon's fist, flat metal end making a perfect arc in the sunlight, glinting malevolently on its way with vicious intent, from that moment everything changed.

At first the cracks were so tiny as to be almost imperceptible. Wheat ripened in the fields around Harry's farm and was harvested with everyone working so hard that the absence of one, two and then four of the business men, previously so keen to help, was scarcely noticed. Sugar beet was lifted and Hilda drove the tractor and trailer until it was all safely stored in the barn. She was still enjoying herself, but had to admit she got very tired,

"Only to be expected at my age," she thought as she dragged herself round to the back of her cottage one autumn evening after a particularly hard day only to find Florence in tears on the doorstep. She stopped dead and pulled off her hat, staring in surprise at the little woman sobbing and blowing her nose.

"Florence, whatever's the matter?"

"Oh, Hilda, it was awful…Minnie said I wasn't running things properly…and all the wool was in a muddle…but the thing was I didn't leave it like that…and she said some of the swaps weren't fair…and nobody knows what they're doing for the Autumn Show…and that some of them got together and decided they want Daphne to take over…"

The sobbing grew to a crescendo as Hilda quickly opened her door and bustled Florence inside. She sat her down and put the kettle on, busying herself with tea things until she could be sure she had composed her face into an expression of sympathy; it wouldn't do to let Florence see that she thought the whole thing too silly for words. As they sipped their tea she had to listen to the tale of how Minnie had been making a nuisance of herself for weeks, nothing much, just little things, running out of wool and hinting that Florence should have seen that coming and made sure they had enough, undermining her in subtle ways.

She dabbed at her eyes with tiny bird-like movements, a spotless, white handkerchief clutched in small, bony fingers. Then she stood, breathing in, holding herself erect with as much dignity as she could muster and tweaked the edges of her lemon sweater down over her sensible tweed skirt.

"Well, I shan't go back. Let Daphne take over."

Hilda followed her to the door and just as she thought they were safely through the crisis, Florence leaned against the wall and crumpled; the tears started again as she turned towards Hilda, handkerchief clutched to her mouth,

"The thing is, Hilda…the thing is…I miss my grandchildren so!"

Hilda managed to get her friend to one of the four chairs around her kitchen table and waited until her shoulders stopped shaking and the dabbing started again, then she said, very gently,

"Florence we all miss people from the other side of the wall, but you know what we agreed; we have to get on with things as they are; we have to survive. It's not as if we have a choice."

"I know…I know…the damned wall! My little granddaughters there on the other side of it…but why haven't they come looking for me? Why hasn't my daughter been to find out what's going on? I shall probably never see them again. It was only fun at first…a challenge…because let's face it, Hilda, we all thought it would go away. At first we were glad just to be alive, then we were glad to be able to survive…until the wall went away. But it's not going to is it? It's not going away."

She lifted her tear-stained face towards her friend and Hilda saw her grief, felt her pain. Tired as she was, her heart went out to her friend, mourning the loss of the two dainty little girls skipping up the path to see their Gran. She remembered watching with more than a tinge of envy as Florence scooped them up, one by one, kissing their blond curls before taking them inside to see what treats she had for them.

Composed now, Florence stood again and walked towards the door. She opened it, then turned back to Hilda,

"Let's face it, if we had a choice, you would probably opt for keeping the wall. I think you're happier than you were before. Anyway…thank-you for listening – and the knitting group can go hang."

She closed the door quietly and Hilda went back into her sitting room sinking gratefully into her favourite chair. It was true. She realised with a shock that what Florence said was quite true. Who did she have on the other side of the wall? There was a divorced nephew and his son who lived in Canada, but apart from that no-one. She had never married and her brother had died years ago. She hadn't seen her nephew for years and since the wall and her involvement with the farm she had been happier than she could remember. Her career had been fun, working as a secretary for some lovely people all over the world. She had even lied about her age once to secure a particularly desirable job in Monaco, but that had all finished years ago. No, since she had retired life had certainly not been fun – until the wall. She felt useful now, part of things again and the two little Gibbons boys, Sam and Nick, had adopted her as their Gran. She looked forward to the days when they were released from school and could work on the farm. She loved to see them racing each other round the corner towards her, shouting and laughing. They were little monkeys, mind, and had to be kept in order, but Jane, their Mum reckoned that Hilda was one of the few people they would listen to,

"…and they do miss their Gran," she had confided, "so I'm really grateful to you for filling that gap for them, just till the wall goes, of course."

"Yes, of course. You can leave them with me during the day; they're no trouble, are you boys?"

And she had hugged them, secretly hoping the wall would never go.

'THE BUBBLE'

Claudia Golightly stretched her hands out in front of her and wiggled her fingers, admiring the shining, bright pink polish freshly painted onto each almond shaped nail and already drying quite quickly in the warmth of the summer house.

"Oh, I love it," she breathed, with a smile, leaning back and enjoying the sensation of hot, scented water in the footbath gently vibrating beneath her feet.

Patti folded a clean, white towel and smoothed it across her lap indicating that she was ready for a foot and Claudia obligingly lifted the right one out, placing it carefully on the towel. As she worked, massaging the dainty toes in front of her with gorgeous, thick cream then shaping the tiny nails, she listened to Claudia talking, mainly about Jack and his influence in her life, but also about her marriage to Gordon and the problems of being stepmother to his two sons.

"Of course it feels like just one at the moment as Nigel was away when the wall came, so we've only got Jeremy. It makes one wonder if we shall ever see anyone again…you know, from the other side of the wall. Mind you, it does mean that one doesn't have to spend so much time socialising with people one would really rather not see, you know, flying here, there and everywhere. Though there are some people who miss their relatives dreadfully. Thank God for Jack, you know, keeping us upbeat and all that."

Patti smiled, but thought she would probably scream if she heard Jack's virtues extolled once more. It was bad enough listening to Giles after he'd been to Church on Sunday mornings running on about the value of Spiritual Development and how we'd all been chasing the wrong things before the wall. As far as she was concerned, life before the wall had suited her nicely, thank-you-very-much, and the sooner the dratted thing came down, or went away, the better.

Suddenly Claudia leaned forward and, looking serious, said, very softly,

"You know, if I'm being really honest and I had to choose, I'd actually rather like the wall to stay."

She giggled and put a freshly manicured hand over her mouth,

"Does that sound really awful?" Without waiting for Patti to answer she went on quickly, as though feeling she ought to justify such a statement.

"It's just that I have everything I want here,"

She waved a tiny hand towards the summer house door and both women looked out across the swimming pool, blue and sparkling in the autumn sunshine, and the green rolling lawns to the mansion beyond.

"I have my horses; it's been such fun teaching some of the children to ride and getting to know the people in the village. We never seemed to have the chance before. But best of all, I see much more of Gordon now; before the wall he was always preoccupied with deals, always away somewhere, now there's nowhere for him to go and we are much happier."

Patti murmured something and bent her head low over Claudia's foot. She daren't look up and tried not to think about Sunday mornings, fearing that her guilt would somehow emblazon itself all over her face. She had resisted for a very long time – well it seemed a long time to her – and had enjoyed Gordon's attempts at seduction, especially as he was trying so hard not to let Claudia see what he was up to. She had ignored the surreptitious brushing of his hand against her backside while taking her coat on those occasions when she and Giles had been invited for drinks; and the suggestive remarks, whispered wetly in her ear, accompanied by a schoolboy snuffle. He was attractive, but definitely past his best, and to say that his approach lacked subtlety was an understatement. There was an air of desperation about him which increased her amusement and she was just biding her time before telling him to get lost.

But it was that damned silly summer barbecue at the river pool in July that had made her change her mind. Giles had insisted on going, even though she didn't want to, and his boyish enthusiasm for the whole thing had made her want to curl up and crawl away somewhere. He was shouting and splashing about with the

Thompson boys all afternoon, he and John Thompson making idiots of themselves on that ridiculous tyre on a rope they had fixed up over the water.

And then when the food was ready, the two of them had organised everyone with the heartiness of scoutmasters at some sort of jamboree, handing out giant burgers and hotdogs, all the while laughing at nothing in particular. She had noticed that Claudia was there chatting to the Thompson woman for most of the afternoon, but she hadn't seen Gordon.

She had sat quietly seething at the stupidity of it all, her knees clasped to her chest, lips resting gently against them until Giles had flung himself down beside her and tried to force her to eat a disgusting looking hot dog. She had said no, quite firmly then, thinking he was being funny, he had said,

"I know what you'd like, my love," and had scooped her up and jumped into the water with her. Everyone had clapped and laughed, and, as she had come up spluttering, she had managed a smile, mainly for Kylie's sake as she saw her daughter watching from the bank. Giles really thought he'd been clever and even tried to splash her as she clambered out of the water, but when everyone's attention was turned away and he tried to help her dry herself she'd told him to bugger off. She had made her way home as quickly as she could after that, telling Kylie that she had a headache.

And it was on the way home that she decided if schoolboy pranks were all she had to look forward to with Giles, she may as well have some adult fun.

Gordon was delighted, of course, couldn't believe his luck when she had whispered in his ear and told him to make his way over the fields one Sunday morning and come in the back way. She had made sure the double entendre was not lost on him as she knew it would appeal to his lewd sense of humour and help to get him excited. She had let him believe she was up for anything, but would be sure to remain in control when the time came.

As she thought he would be, Gordon was a poor lover, rough and lacking in finesse. He belonged to that body of men who believe it's all about push and power. Thrust away and if the poor mare doesn't enjoy it, well there's something wrong with her. Patti managed to slow him down for long enough to make sure it wasn't a complete disaster for her, and they both got enough out of the experience to want the affair to continue; it was their Sunday morning answer to Church. In fact it was because of Church that they didn't have to worry about being discreet. Gordon continued to walk over the fields – no point in taking unnecessary risks – but with practically the whole population of the village sitting listening to the wonderful Jack or boring old Mervyn there was little chance that they would be discovered.

Gordon's approach to mating meant that time was not an issue; he had always finished and departed before Giles and Kylie arrived home.

Claudia leaned forward again, dark hair falling around her beautiful face, and whispered,

"Actually, I don't know why, but things are much better in bed with Gordon these days," she gave a throaty giggle and blushed, "...he just seems more tender and considerate somehow...Oh, I'm sorry, that was my fault, I'm embarrassing you."

She looked in dismay at the shiny, pink blob of polish that had fallen on the white towel and held her foot still while Patti quickly removed the smudged varnish from her big toe.

"No...sorry...it's me who should apologise...how very clumsy. Sorry Claudia; I'll start again with that nail and don't worry about the towel, I've got plenty more."

"No, I insist on replacing it. I shouldn't have said anything about our sex life...but when things improve you want to tell someone, don't you?"

"Of course," Patti said, now fully in control of herself, "It's just that Giles and I are going through a bit of a bad patch at the moment and we..."

"Oh, Patti, I'm so sorry. I wouldn't have said anything if I'd known."

"It's fine. I'm sure things will sort themselves out."

With the job finished, she sat back and Claudia, exquisite hazel eyes full of concern, slipped her tiny feet carefully into flip-flops,

"Come up to the house and we'll have a lovely lunch with some of Gordon's best wine before you go back home."

She pushed the summer house chairs into place with her back turned, so didn't see Patti packing her equipment with sharp, staccato movements, her lips drawn into a tight, thin line. 'Damn Gordon…damn his eyes!' Brief though their encounters were, and however much she had tried to focus on his inadequacies, she hadn't realised how much she had started to entertain the idea that she may perhaps become more to him than just a casual fling. She stood on the steps waiting for Claudia to lock the summer house and looked around. Yes, if she was honest, she had begun to hope that all this could be hers one day – she had no way of knowing that most of it belonged to Claudia. Giles hadn't come near her since she had walked away from that stupid barbecue and, crude though Gordon's love-making was it was better than nothing, especially as she thought she had started to improve things in that department.

But all the while he was telling her that he and Claudia weren't sleeping together, he was using her to slake his lust so that he could afford to focus more on his wife's pleasure when they were in bed. She really was just his bit on the side.

Claudia slipped her hand through Patti's arm and they walked together across the beautiful lawn.

"Now, in the spirit of the way we operate these days, you must tell me what I have to give you in exchange for the manicure and pedicure."

Patti glanced at the animated face of the person next to her, dark hair blowing across her cheeks, and felt really guilty. It was impossible to dislike Claudia Golightly, and she didn't deserve the treatment she was getting from Gordon – the infidelity which she was making possible. Suddenly she hated him. She smiled at Claudia and said,

"It sounds as though the lunch you have promised me will do nicely."

Claudia opened her mouth to protest, but Patti insisted, her mind already starting to focus on how she was going to get rid of Gordon.

By the end of September fruits had been gathered all over the three villages and jars of varying sizes filled with jams, chutneys and pickles to be shared, swapped and displayed with pride at both the Autumn Show and the Harvest Festival. Both of these events promised to be bigger and better this year than ever before as there were more people entering, more with time to take part. The best vegetables were lovingly nurtured for this purpose and the rest picked and eaten, or frozen for future use; while on Harry's farm work progressed steadily as before,

"Now what we gotta do," said Harry lugubriously to his willing crew of workers, is spread some o' that pigs' muck on the land before we plough."

A few made faces but accepted that the less pleasant, smelly jobs had to be done; it wasn't all hay making and gathering corn in the sunshine, so for the most part they set to work with enthusiasm. Soon Harry would show them how to plough and harrow the land ready to drill the winter corn and the whole process would start again.

In the kitchen at Holly Tree House Rebekka and Kylie were carefully assembling all the utensils they needed to make skin cream – well Rebekka was; Kylie seemed more interested in staring out of the window while absent-mindedly sucking a strand of hair.

"Come on, Kylie, we need to get all the ingredients together as well."

Her friend jumped down from the stool and, swinging her hair back over her shoulder started helping to put the little jars, bottles and packages together on the work top. Cocoa butter ('Mmmm that smells yummy'), Macadamia Nut oil, Thistle Oil,

Apricot Oil, Cetyl Alcohol, ('Hey, do you think we could drink that, Bekks?' 'No'), VE Emulsifier, Spring Water, Glycerine and Essential Oils.

They pored over pans, pots and bowls with the dedication of scientists about to make a significant discovery, one that would change the world. With furrowed brows and bottom lips held anxiously between teeth they measured, mixed, blended and stirred.

Rebekka screwed the lid onto a jar and carefully added one of the labels she had made earlier.

"And who would have thought we could have got all this from 'Mad Martha.'"

"Yeah, it's weird isn't it? She's really nice, not at all the scatty old woman we thought she was; and her house is lovely – full of treasures from top to bottom – and so clean with everything neatly arranged."

"And the scent. Every room smells of perfume, did you notice?"

"I did." Kylie paused and looked up, "Actually, I meant to tell you, I asked her if she would teach us to make that too – for the swap shop – and she said she would."

"Oh, stormin'! That'll be great."

Suddenly Rebekka stopped what she was doing and took hold of Kylie's left hand.

"Where is it?"

Kylie blushed and looked down, snatching her hand away quickly and putting it behind her back.

"Why aren't you wearing it, Kylie?"

Suddenly angry, Kylie looked up at her friend,

"Because I'm not! What are you my mother now?"

The room was silent apart from the ticking of the old clock in the corner. Rebekka spoke softly,

"But we said we would. We told Jack…"

"Don't talk to me about Jack! I don't want to hear his name…"

She spat the words out, then suddenly crumpled and buried her head in her hands, as her shoulders shook with sobs and tears started to run out between her fingers.

"Oh, Kylie what's the matter? What is it?"

Rebekka put her arms around her friend and cradled her head against her shoulder until the tears subsided and she blew her nose noisily.

"Oh Bekks, I wanted to tell you everything…it's just that I felt so confused."

Rebekka led her to the sofa by the window,

"Look, you sit there and I'll get us some mint tea. Then you can tell me. O.K?"

"O.K."

Rebekka filled the kettle and, as she waited for it to boil, looked at the ring on the index finger of her left hand, a pretty band of twisted silver, and thought back to the warm Sunday in June when Jack had given it to her. He had been preaching about the sanctity of marriage and she and Kylie had dared each other to ask him if he thought all sex before marriage was wrong. They had, she remembered, giggled a lot as they walked along, arm in arm, wondering where they could find him. They hadn't been able to ask him at the Church door as there were too many people about and when they had looked round he had gone, they didn't see which way. Just as they were about to give up on the whole idea he suddenly appeared, walking beside them and this, of course made them dissolve into a further a fit of giggles. Jack had waited patiently until the giggles subsided and said,

"Is there something you want to ask me?"

They had no idea how he could possibly know, but Kylie, keen to impress him, had plucked up the courage and asked him the question. There followed a serious discussion during which it became clear that Jack did indeed believe in girls keeping themselves pure for the man they would eventually marry, and when they arrived at the gate to Holly Tree House both girls were amazed when he turned towards them with two pretty silver rings in the palm of his hand.

"Wear these as a sign that you will keep yourselves pure for your marriage. Put them on the index fingers of your left hands and don't take them off."

They had heard about these rings being worn by girls in America years ago, but hadn't been particularly interested. It seemed so old fashioned somehow and Kylie in particular hadn't been at all impressed by the idea of purity, but if Jack said it was how things should be then that was different. They had taken the rings and gently eased them onto their fingers where they fitted perfectly and shone in the sun. They held up their hands, their faces flushed and smiling, watching the rings glitter and gleam, but when they had turned to thank Jack, he had gone.

Kylie had twirled and danced her way up the drive, declaring that she would never take hers off, ever!

Rebekka handed her friend the tea and sat down next to her on the sofa. She looked out of the window, sipped and waited until Kylie looked up and spoke slowly,

"Everything was O.K. until the day of that dratted summer barbecue, you know down at the river pool..."

"Oh yeah...I remember...I thought it was great...Oh, sorry Kylie."

Rebekka sipped her tea silently and allowed her friend to continue.

"Oh yeah, it was great fun, until I saw my mum and dad...they didn't exactly have a row and mum tried really hard not to let me see she was upset, but I knew she was. I think it was because dad jumped in the pool with her," Rebekka nodded but didn't interrupt, "then she said she had headache and went home. Anyway I went, too, soon after that as I wanted to make sure she was O.K. and on the way I did what I had often started to do."

Here Kylie paused and looked out of the window. Rebekka waited until she continued,

"I went through Martha's orchard..." She looked straight at Rebekka, "I went through Martha's orchard because it's the only place I've ever seen Jack, except for Church and meetings and things, so I used to go there, hoping I'd see him. And that day I did."

Kylie paused and sipped her tea.

"I saw him sitting very still with his back leaning against a tree and I went and sat down beside him. Without even opening his eyes he said, 'Hello, Kylie' and honestly, Bekks, I just melted. I thought it was a sign or something and I told him how I felt. I said I loved him and that I was wearing the ring and keeping myself pure just for him. I was longing to hear him say he felt the same, but he opened his eyes – those beautiful eyes so full of kindness and compassion – and told me that it could never be. He said it so gently, but that made it worse, somehow; it was final. I think he wanted to say more, but I felt so humiliated, I just got up and ran.

When I got home I pulled off the ring and threw it as hard as I could out of the window; then mum and dad started screaming at each other so I just had to get out of the house. I walked to the wall and sat there looking out; there was no-one else around…and then Simon arrived." She paused again and Rebekka frowned,

Simon? Who, Simon Brown?"

"Yes."

"Simon Brown who works for Ernie Briggs?"

"Yes, Bekks. Simon Brown who works for Ernie Briggs. You know he's been after me for ages."

"Yes, I know but you said…we both said…"

"It doesn't matter what we said. That was before." Kylie snapped, then went on quickly,

"We chatted for a while; he was very kind and gentle, he said he had seen me heading towards the wall and thought I looked upset, so he followed me. Anyway he walked me home and asked me out…I've been seeing him ever since."

Kylie's voice had tailed off and she looked down, but then her head jerked up; she looked straight at Rebekka and said, defiantly,

"And as for the stupid old purity rings…well, as far as I'm concerned they are for babies and immature girls who are too scared to have a bit of fun!"

Rebekka gasped,

"Kylie…you haven't…you don't mean you've…with Simon Brown!?"

"Yes I have! And more than once if you want to know!"

She leapt up and grabbed her jacket, pulling it savagely around her shoulders,

"…And as that obviously shocks you, little Miss Purity, I shall go."

She flicked her blond hair over her shoulder and flounced out leaving Rebekka sitting on the sofa staring after her.

'THE BUBBLE'

Chapter Seventeen

By mid October, as shadows lengthened and leaves turned from green to gold trembling in a wind that carried with it more than a hint of winter chill to follow, the cracks in the perfect world behind the wall were so much in evidence they could no longer be ignored. The ladies knitting circle had all but broken up; and many of the bakers had declared that they would no longer bake for the people in the villages but, henceforth, only for their own families. The number of Harry's helpers had dwindled to the point where the remaining workers felt put upon – too much to do and too few people willing to pull their weight; and at the school Carolyn was getting complaints now about the way she was running things,

"...Bit more book learnin,' that's what they need. They got too much freedom, won't do 'em no good when the wall comes down and they have to cope in the real world..."

"Can't they see that this is the real world now? Their children will survive – they have the skills they need to live the life we now have. I mean...if it should ever change, we don't know what we'd find out there and we'll just have to cross that bridge when we come to it. The point is they are confident and curious, they have the basics and the right attitude to be able to learn anything. We have taught them to learn about learning, how to go about acquiring any knowledge or skills they need"

Carolyn was sitting on a bale in the barn venting her frustration on the tightly packed straw which she was pulling out in small clumps and twisting in her fingers. She was watching John plane a piece of wood and the rhythmic movement, calm and steady, was helping to soothe her. They were alone, the boys were out delivering a finished gate, and the warm October sun filtered in through the open door. Outside she could see their chickens scratching lazily in the dusty ground and hear the pigs snuffling in their sty. She smiled as one of them stuck a wet, pink snout over the top to see what was going on. The large vegetable patch looked quite bare now as the onions had been pulled, dried in the sunshine and plaited before being hung up to store; carrots and parsnips had been put into trays of sand, and potatoes into clamps. The densely tangled foliage of the runner beans and mass of green tendrils which had yielded such a pleasing crop of peas were all down, and much of the waste that couldn't be composted had been burned on large, satisfying bonfires, from which tendrils of smoke still drifted long after the flames had gone.

Carolyn sighed,

"I wish people could see that this place is going to be just as good or bad as we make it. The strange thing is, I think everyone did see that at first, but with the passage of time life as it was before the wall is being invested with a glamour it never possessed. And I for one don't want it back."

She seemed almost surprised at what she was hearing herself say and looked at her husband.

"Do you?"

"Oh no." John paused, and straightened up, "No, I don't want it back. As far as I'm concerned the life I've got now is as near to paradise as I'm ever likely to find this side of the grave."

He smiled at his wife, pleased to see she was looking a little calmer; she had always been sensitive, it was one of the things he loved about her, but it did make her vulnerable. She felt things too keenly. He bent to continue his planing and Carolyn said softly,

"Actually, it's strange you should mention the grave, John. Have you noticed that no-one has died since the wall came? Richard Clegg has been tending the vegetables in the open areas all over the village as he's had no-one to bury for ten months."

John paused again and thought for a moment, then said with a slight frown,

"Yes…yes, you're right. It seems that old Martha's lotions and potions are keeping everyone healthy; the nurses down at the health centre seem happy with them anyway. Oh well, don't knock it." And he resumed his planing.

It was also noticeable that the congregations in all three churches had fallen off quite significantly. People no longer seemed to feel the need for spiritual sustenance in the way they had at first, and alternative activities were claiming them; though none as potentially disturbing as the very exclusive club that met on Sunday mornings in Gordon Golightly's drawing room.

His affair with Patti had finished, and if he was honest he was feeling quite relieved about this; in fact he couldn't quite believe his luck. She had become a bit too clingy for his liking – always put him off when they started doing that, calling him 'darling' and wanting more foreplay before getting down to the action. He had been wondering how to get rid of her without risking the 'woman scorned' bit, which could send her scuttling down to tell Claudia what they'd been up to, when she sent him packing. It was after she'd been down to The Manor to give Claudia some kind of beauty treatment – apparently this was her contribution to the new life, the only thing she could do really, as she certainly had no brains.

He had to admit he had been a bit concerned when Claudia had told him about it at breakfast,

"...Patti O'Dell, you know, darling, Giles' wife...they've been here for drinks...anyway, before the wall she owned beauty salons in London so she's coming down to give me a manicure and pedicure. We'll go in the summer house by the pool if the weather's nice..."

He needn't have worried. All Claudia could talk about after the session was how sorry she felt for poor Patti as she and Giles weren't getting on too well. Hardly surprising really as she was screwing him, not much left for the poor bastard. Anyway the very next week she said she didn't want to see him any more as she realised she was no more to him than a bit on the side. Well, he could have told her that. What did she expect? He had managed to hide his relief and pretended to be upset at the prospect of not seeing her again...thought that the best way as it would let her think she was in control and stop her from blabbing. It would also allow him to put into practice a little plan that had been rattling around in his brain ever since that day in July when he had tried to flatten Jack with a spade.

Gordon had noticed that everything in paradise was not quite what it had been. He had found Jeremy lounging around by the pool when he was supposed to be at Harry's farm and asked him why he wasn't down there; he'd seemed quite keen at first, inasmuch as Jeremy was ever keen on anything.

"Too much like bloody slave labour – a hell of a lot of work to do and not enough of us to do it."

He had rolled over lazily on the lounger, and Gordon sat down on a nearby chair.

"I thought you said the place was crawling with people all keen to get their hands dirty."

"And so it was, at first. I think a lot of them have got fed up with it, though, they want their old lives back with all the stresses and strains; it's what they were used to. They're fed up with scratching around in the mud."

Gordon was interested,

"Who exactly is fed up with scratching around in the mud?"

"Oh, I don't know…the captains of industry mainly I suppose…you know the ones who were getting towards the top of the ladder…looking forward to retirement, thinking they would enjoy a bit of country life even though they'd never really tried it. Well…novelty's worn off and they think maybe their old life wasn't so bad after all. Their idea of country life was a few rounds of golf and the rest of the day getting out of their heads on gin. When the wall came they thought they were sort of holding the fort until it went and they could look back and boast about their little interludes as peasants. Have their fifteen minutes of fame, you know come out of it all smelling of roses, not pig shit. I don't think they expected to be at it for so long. Let's face it, none of us did."

He leaned up on one elbow,

"They want their pensions and their cruises. Can't blame them, can you? I will also be mightily glad when the bloody wall goes and I can get away from this hell hole."

Gordon was no longer listening to the whining of his elder son; he was thinking…planning…delighted to know that the simpering Simpson and blustering Cunningham were, potentially, not his only allies. He stood up,

"You don't happen to have any names do you, old son, of these 'captains of industry?'"

'Oh, god…' Jeremy rolled onto his back and managed to scrape together half a dozen, pleased to see that reeling them off to his old man had the desired effect of making him clear off,

"Thanks, Jem…and by the way try not to swear so much…very unbecoming."

"Bloody old hypocrite," Jeremy muttered as he closed his eyes and stretched out in the sun.

It had been easy after that, going round to the executive residences in all three villages, knocking on doors and inviting the old duffers down for a drink on Sunday morning.

"Thought you might need cheering up, old boy, I do still have some rather fine French brandy left and…well, in these strange times…may as well enjoy it…"

"I say, Gordon, jolly decent of you…yes, why not. I'm sure the memsahib won't mind missing Church for once, doesn't seem quite so keen these days…"

But Gordon managed to persuade them all that the order of the day was really 'chaps only', not that they needed much persuading as a few bevies in a woman free environment was something they were sorely missing from the days before the wall.

It all worked out exactly as he had planned. Word spread and the number of men in Gordon's little gatherings grew over the weeks; it soon became the place to be on Sunday mornings – if you could get in – as attendance was by invitation only.

Once they were there, faces ruddy and glowing from too much booze, mellowing in the ambience of a palatial drawing room, the air of which they had no qualms about polluting with cigar smoke, it was an easy matter for Gordon to drop his hints. He made sure that every whinge and whine could be attributed to something that Jack had said or done. The more the brandy flowed the less likely it was that anyone would bother to question the truth of the innuendo and there were nods of agreement accompanied by murmurs of

"...quite right, old chap, the man's a menace."

It wasn't even a problem if they weren't gone by the time Claudia returned from Church as she didn't seem to mind. She was a little taken aback the first time she had walked in on an exclusively male gathering in her smoke-filled drawing room at midday on a Sunday. She had laughed nervously and looked anxiously round for Gordon who had appeared immediately by her side.

"I hope you don't mind, darling, a few friends have dropped in for a drink. They won't stay long. Is it alright?"

It was Gordon at his most charming, though without the rose-tinted spectacles of love, some would have called it slimy. Claudia was charmed and said that of course it was alright for him to entertain friends; in fact she was secretly quite glad as she had worried a little in the past that he didn't seem to have many friends, but now...just another good effect of the wall as far as she was concerned.

Gordon had made an exaggerated show of kissing her and enjoyed the envious eyes of his 'friends' on him as he did so, knowing the stout, comely matrons or ageing stick insects that most of them would go home to. No wonder they watched his beautiful, softly curving wife as she walked quickly across the lawn towards the stables to help tend and exercise her beloved horses until it was time for dinner, which they would eat together in the cool of the evening, when all the old bores had gone.

It was, Gordon knew, necessary to curry favour with the wives as well, and the opportunity to do so presented itself at the Autumn Show. Following the success of his Sunday morning drinking sessions, he had found it quite easy to begin influencing the decisions made at the Monday meetings. The wretched things, flaming nuisance as far as he was concerned (certainly while Jack's word prevailed as law in everything) could now be turned to his advantage. He only had to wink at a few of his cronies and, eagerly anticipating their next Sunday male bonding session, they voted any way he wanted. They exuded confidence and many of the now disgruntled villagers started to follow them; so when Gordon put himself forward as the judge for The Show, he was voted in with quite a significant majority, in spite of the fact that Jack said it would be nice if the honour was shared.

Carolyn frowned and looked around, feeling very uncomfortable about the way things were going. Had people forgotten what Gordon Golightly was really like?

He was in his element on the day of The Show, striding around in cavalry twills, mustard waistcoat, tweed jacket and matching trilby, prodding the ground with a very showy, silver-headed walking cane. People seemed to be regarding him with a new respect, watching in silence as he passed judgement on floral arrangements, cakes, home made jams and vegetables. Ladies twittered nervously as he sampled their Victoria sponges,

"…lovely, my dear, a culinary treat, absolutely light as a feather…"

He mumbled between bites, crumbs dropping to the floor of the marquee and jam clinging to his lower lip in tiny, sticky blobs to be lifted off with a podgy finger and sucked in to his mouth, smiling all the while at the hopeful contestant. She smiled back, fidgeting nervously, fingers twisting together, unaware that the winner was already decided. He regarded floral arrangements, about which he knew absolutely nothing, with the seriousness of an expert, brow a little furrowed, standing back, then moving forward again and peering intently at flowers and foliage. Giant marrows, polished and gleaming, small groups of green and white leeks, perfectly formed carrots and brown papery onions all received the same treatment; so no-one would have guessed, in fact it would have been churlish beyond words to even think that it was anything other than pure coincidence that all the winners were either members, or related to members, of Gordon's exclusive club. It was cheers and smiles all round as worthy ladies and pink-faced men walked up to receive their trophies – all kindly donated by Gordon, of course. There were a few raised eyebrows and just one or two murmurs from the former members of the knitting group who felt sure that Daphne's outstanding flower arrangement and Minnie's cake were actually in a different league from the ones that won, but who were they to question the likes of Gordon Golightly.

Chapter Eighteen

After The Show people's thoughts turned quite naturally towards Christmas, the first Christmas behind the wall, and for a while it looked as though the community spirit, which had so fired everyone at first, may be returning – it was, after all, Christmas.

The bakers drifted back to work to produce Christmas puddings and rich, fruit-filled cakes along with the usual loaves; children made decorations and the ladies' knitting circle, re-formed in honour of the season, turned their hands to producing cards and even calendars, though some wondered why these were needed; after all it was not as if they could plan holidays, visits to relatives or business meetings. Any arrangements made now were fairly casual… 'We'll fetch your gate along the day after tomorrow'… but most felt it was still necessary to record the passing of time.

Parties were planned and everyone dug out as many decorations as they could find; it was as though it had become more necessary than ever in the prevailing uncertainty to cling to something that could be universally recognised as normal. And Christmas was Christmas, firmly rooted and unchanging.

Kylie and Rebekka worked even harder at the swap shop, persuading everyone to bring along garments that were glamorous or glittery and they re-made them. They held a successful Christmas fashion show; the boy band, sardonically named 'Off the Wall,' played during the evening while men, women, boys and girls of all ages, including a reluctant Carolyn, strutted their stuff along the catwalk. The girls had put together outfits for James, Jake and the other two lads, and everyone agreed the group looked and sounded good.

The rift between Kylie and Rebekka had healed quite quickly. In her heart of hearts Kylie knew that she was more than a little ashamed of herself and, not feeling nearly as confident about the way she was behaving as she tried to appear, she had taken it out on her friend. But she missed her. Bekks was her steadying influence in a life that was otherwise built on shifting sand, and she couldn't bear to lose her. Rebekka, too, was glad when an envelope came through the letter box with Kylie's writing on it. Life was far too quiet without her zany friend and she smiled when she read the little note which said,

'Sorry, Babe. I'm a silly cow; forgive me and let's talk.

Love, Kylie.

She did, of course, forgive her and they talked. Kylie admitted that sex with Simon Brown wasn't really much fun. It had hurt the first time, though she had tried not to let him know that it was the first time but she thought he must have guessed, and after that it just didn't seem to mean anything.

"The trouble is, while we're doing it I just keep imagining that he's Jack."

Kylie blushed as she confessed this and Rebekka felt sorry for her. She said, very gently,

"It's not fair, really is it?"

"No, I know. I shall have to give him up, but I'm dreading it. What if he turns nasty? I mean we know, don't we…like we said, he is a bit of a slob…oh he's quite kind and all that, and he does try, but we can't really talk about anything." She looked miserable and Rebekka muttered,

"No…I can imagine."

Though imagining her friend with Simon Brown was something she preferred not to do.

For Gordon, basking in his growing popularity, the silly season was providing an effective smoke screen. With a jolly expression on his face, which he donned like a mask when in company, he went about being pleasant to everyone, but all the while watching and waiting for the opportunity to topple Jack once and for all. Carol Services and special services for children were arranged – of course they were it was Christmas – there had to be a Christingle Service, a Crib Service and a Midnight Mass. Mince pies and mulled wine would be served, all the traditions observed, and the bells would ring out on Christmas morning.

'THE BUBBLE'

The bells…the bells…Gordon listened to them pealing out one cold, frosty evening as the ringers held their weekly practice and the germ of an idea began to form in his mind. They would ring on New Year's Eve…they would ring in 2021, then after that they would continue to disturb the peace – flaming nuisance as far as he was concerned – every Tuesday evening. Peter Cunningham was the Tower Captain…so could he…was it possible that…?

The idea took shape and grew. He poured himself a large brandy, so pleased was he with his ingenuity, and the self congratulatory drink helped him to put the finishing touches to a plan; a plan so vile it could only have been dreamt up by someone like Gordon Golightly but, sadly, if executed with skill and precision it could work, and it would look like an accident.

As Gordon predicted he would, Peter thought the idea a brilliant one; of all his new found 'friends' he and Clive were still the only two who knew that Gordon's hatred of Jack extended to thoughts of murder, but Clive was not party to this discussion. When Peter, summoned to The Manor one cold, dark evening, had asked if they were waiting for him, Gordon had put an arm around his shoulder and, with an expression of extreme concern on his face, had said he felt that perhaps it would put too much of a strain on 'the poor chap…if you know what I mean,.' and continued with a conspiratorial wink, 'not made of quite the same stuff as you and me, old boy.'

"Quite so…quite so…know just what you mean, mate. Wouldn't want to get him into bother with Norma, would we?" And Peter gave a bark of laughter, flattered by being in league with a man like Gordon, and totally unaware of just how much he was despised by him. They went over the plan again and Cunningham reassured Gordon he was definitely up for it,

"…trust me, mate, I hate him as much as you do, and I can do it. No sweat."

Then he slid away into the night. Gordon was well pleased. There was no reason why his plan shouldn't work and with Jack and the Church both gone he was contemplating a New Year with things getting back to the way he wanted.

Buoyed up and carried along by anticipating the success of his plan, Gordon was able to throw himself into the Christmas celebrations with so much enthusiasm it almost looked genuine. Claudia was helping at the lunch being held in the Village Hall by the members of the knitting group, and when Minnie asked if Gordon would do them the honour of being Father Christmas she said she was sure he would – and he did. Guffawing loudly and handing out gifts to all the old dears, he even allowed them to kiss him, amid much ooooing and aaahing, relieved that they were unable to see the expression of disgust on his face and also heartily glad that there was enough cotton wool to shield him from the dribbly kisses.

This honour was not repeated at the school where the part of Father Christmas was played by a genuinely benevolent and smiling Harry Frost. The snub wasn't lost on Gordon who had, for some time, been slightly unsettled by Carolyn who he thought of as 'that Thompson woman.' She always looked at him as though she could see right through him, and when he had once slid his arm round her at a social gathering – just being friendly, of course, – she had pulled away as though stung by some repulsive insect, and given him a withering look, before walking quickly away to join her boring husband. He made a mental note to bring her down a peg or two under the new regime.

The Christmas Concerts at the school were a great success. Maggie and Jenny worked hard to make sure that the singing and dancing were truly stunning, and they were delighted when Jack asked Carolyn if the children would perform in Church so that everyone, not just the proud parents, would be able to enjoy such an uplifting experience. They did, and Carolyn, moved to tears as were many of the congregation, really felt that the people in the three villages were well on the way to recovering the community spirit they had discovered initially, and that 2021 would see them thriving again.

At Midnight Mass the Church was packed. Everyone gazed in wonder at the transformation wrought by candles as hundreds of them glowed and flickered from every available surface. There was greenery, dark and sweet-smelling; a huge tree which John and the boys, assisted by Brian, Harry, Ernie, David and many others had manoeuvred into place then watched, sipping coffee, as Rebekka and Kylie supervised the decorating. Children scrambled about putting glittering baubles on the lower branches but had to be pulled off the ladder so that adults could climb up to trim the higher ones, then place a fairy on the very top.

Brasses gleamed and woodwork shone, even to the rafters where Angels with huge wings carved out of oak looked down over folded hands. Everyone tumbled out into the frosty air, warmed by mulled wine and wished each other 'Happy Christmas' before heading towards home.

On Christmas morning the bells pealed out across the fields and Claudia was quite surprised to see Gordon smiling as though he was enjoying the sound. She had noticed how much he had changed recently and was delighted; he seemed to be making such an effort to be pleasant to everyone – she was even secretly hoping she might get him along to Church, but softly, softly. She didn't think he was quite ready for that yet, though when Jack had asked if he would read at the Carol Service she noticed he had thought hard about it before declining, quite graciously, saying that others who attended regularly should really have that honour. She was so proud of his consideration and thoughtfulness that when he suggested a little siesta that afternoon she was more than happy to oblige.

It was also lovely to see the way everyone was looking out for each other again. She and Carolyn Thompson had talked about this while they were making discreet enquiries to ensure that no-one would be alone on Christmas Day, but they needn't have worried as it seemed that everyone who wanted company would have it. Gordon assured her that all his new friends had people to go to, and although Carolyn had tried to persuade Hilda and Florence to go round to Holly Tree House for the day it was to no avail. They agreed to go for a few drinks before lunch, but insisted they would be happy to spend the rest of the day together; though Hilda wasn't sure that 'happy' was the word she would use when Florence started shedding tears over missing her granddaughters. Boxing Day would be better as she knew that Florence, having vowed she wouldn't, had actually made her peace with the ladies in the knitting circle and was invited round to Daphne's house for a day of fun and party games. Hilda had smiled when Florence told her and felt heartily glad that she had her own treat to look forward to; she had been asked to go round to spend the day with her two adopted grandsons, Sam and Nick Gibbons, and there was no way she was missing that.

Christmas Day at Holly Tree House was magical. From the moment she got up until she collapsed into bed well after midnight, Carolyn felt as though she was being carried along on a cloud of pure joy. She had never before known a Christmas quite like it and wondered, strangely, in a quiet moment just after lunch, whether she ever would again. It was another of those rare experiences, like the skylark in the summer, where everything, just for a while comes together and works in such perfect harmony that it seems to transcend reality and the recipient is transported to a higher plane. It is, however tinged with sadness as, by the very nature of the fact that it's perfect, it can't last.

After hot coffee and croissants silly gifts were exchanged, and it was difficult to believe that her children exclaiming with delight over home-made offerings were the same young people who had, in previous years, demanded the very latest and most expensive in technological gadgetry or designer clothes. The boys were thrilled with the sparkly waistcoats and matching bow ties that Rebekka had made for them to wear when playing at birthday parties and other celebrations. They were much in demand in all three villages now and needed several different outfits for the various gigs. Jake even gave his sister a hug then felt embarrassed as he saw John and Carolyn smiling, so he was glad of the chance to escape when James beckoned him outside to fetch Rebekka's present. She was equally delighted with their gift to her, and lovingly stroked the satin smooth wood of the little coffee table made especially for her room. She gave Carolyn a matching set of jewellery she had painstakingly strung together, and for her dad there was a hessian bag of tools acquired at the swap shop. Carolyn had swapped some evening dresses she no longer needed to get John a warm, waterproof coat as he was spending so much time outside these days; and for the boys she had found some old combat trousers she knew they would love.

The gift giving continued with much laughter and everyone marvelling at everyone else's ingenuity, until it was time to get dressed and welcome their guests for drinks. As they had been to Midnight Mass they had decided not to go to Church, so everything was ready by the time Hilda and Florence rang the doorbell. Kylie, of course, had arrived earlier and joined in with the general chaos. She had dispensed gifts to everyone, beside herself with excitement as the boys removed the homemade wrapping paper from theirs to find a bowler hat each to go with their waistcoats,

"They will look stormin' on you. Trust me,"

Kylie shrieked, but James and Jake needed no convincing having already decided that their image would be modelled on a very old jazz band they had seen pictures of in their great grandfather's house before the wall.

Florence and Hilda were very quickly joined by Giles who appeared, much to John's delight, but full of apologies for Patti who didn't as she had a headache. Carolyn wasn't surprised; although she had tried to befriend her, sensing the deep unhappiness in this strangely aloof woman, Patti had not responded. It was, however, with a cry of pure delight that she greeted the arrival of Claudia Golightly,

"Just popping in for a quick drink, darling, and to wish you all a Very Happy Christmas; mustn't stay long as Jeremy and Gordon are expecting lunch at about two.

As it was she did stay for long enough to enjoy a couple of songs sung by Jake, accompanied by James on his new guitar – another Christmas gift courtesy of the swap shop.

The guests departed at midday feeling very mellow, Hilda and Florence walking arm in arm, a little unsteadily, towards the bungalows; Giles and Kylie nipping round the corner and Claudia striding purposefully off across the fields, glad that she'd had the foresight to ask her housekeeper to get lunch underway.

The Thompson family had decided it would be much more fun, and make the most of the day, if they snacked on the nibbles produced to accompany the drinks at lunch time and ate their main meal in the evening. So, wrapped up warmly and well in time to enjoy the bright December sunshine, they set off and walked half the perimeter of the wall, returning as the setting sun threw elongated shadows before them and their breath plumed out in the gathering dusk.

Carolyn couldn't remember them ever before enjoying such a convivial walk and said a silent prayer of thanks as they discarded their outer clothes and helped in various ways to produce the Christmas meal. The turkey had been cooking while they were out, so an hour later they sat down, bathed in the glow of several strategically placed candles, and passed around dishes piled high with good things, all from their own garden. There were roast potatoes cooked to perfection, so crisp and golden on the outsides that a knife had to be tapped quite hard against these shining shells in order to crack them and reveal the hot, steaming fluffiness within. There were roast parsnips, crisp and sticky, and tiny peas, bright green and quite sweet, as well as crunchy orange carrots and small, firm sprouts.

There were two kinds of stuffing, made by John and proudly presented as his piece de resistance, gloopy bread sauce and plenty of thick gravy, piping hot. Everyone was full to bursting, but determined to find room for the pudding, a shining mound, densely packed with fruit and surrounded by flickering blue flames as brandy was poured over it by Jake and ignited by James. They cheered and clapped, rum butter was passed around and everyone declared it was quite the best Christmas dinner ever.

Silver cutlery tapped on plates scraping up the last of the delicious fruit floating in pools of white, sugary butter, while candlelight cast a glow over the beautifully decorated table, sparkling on crystal glasses, investing everyone with an air of mystery, and Carolyn felt a little afraid. It was perfect, too perfect and it was then that she was disturbed again by the same feeling she had experienced that day in the meadow, listening to the skylark. After what must have been only a few moments, but actually felt longer, Jake said something funny and they all laughed. She shook herself and turned her attention to enjoying this time with her family, determined that no silly irrational, morbid thoughts would be allowed to spoil something so special.

After the dinner was cleared away Kylie joined them and they played games, silly, old fashioned ones like charades and sardines and Rebekka wasn't surprised to see James following Kylie out of the room to find out where she was going to hide. She smiled to herself, pleased that maybe her friend would soon have a good reason to tell Simon Brown that she had interests elsewhere. James would be good for Kylie, providing just the sort of steadying influence she needed in her life. He was quiet, unlike Jake, the clown, but certainly not boring; and he was already the brother she turned to when she needed any help or advice.

At the end of the evening Carolyn produced a tray of hot drinks, and after they were all finished, Kylie got up to go and declared it was definitely the best Christmas she had ever had in her entire life,

"…even counting the ones I spent in Florida and the Bahamas…oh and Barbados."

"Well, we're truly honoured," said John with a twinkle, and everyone laughed except James who got up quietly and said he would see Kylie home.

"What? It's only just round the corner, what on earth..." Jake spluttered, but was quickly silenced by looks from both his mother and sister. Finally the penny dropped,

"Oh, I see..."

Carolyn stood up and said quickly,

"Jake come and help me wash up the cups,"

And he followed her obediently into the kitchen, grinning at his elder brother as he passed, while Kylie fastened her coat and hugged Rebekka.

On Boxing Day they relaxed, ate leftovers, played more games and walked, this time all the way round the wall, before collapsing in front of the fire. Kylie joined them again, and Carolyn noticed that she and James were very aware of each other, deliberately sitting together but making it look casual. Like Rebekka, she was glad as she believed Kylie was basically a decent girl who was being damaged by her upbringing. How sad that she didn't want to spend the time with Patti and Giles; one could only imagine the sort of atmosphere that prevailed in the house round the corner, full of every luxury imaginable except human warmth.

The family had decided, like most of the inhabitants of the three villages, to award themselves a holiday during the period between Christmas and New year, but with no-where to go and no-one to provide entertainment for them they had to create a holiday at home.

For the girls there were long scented baths by candlelight and plenty of time to spend curled up in front of the fire with books. Everyone laughed themselves silly at old films, as televisions functioned well enough to be used with DVD players, even though they couldn't receive information from the world outside. A golf course of sorts had been developed over a couple of fields in Upper West Side and John and the boys joined others from the three villages, both men and women, to play golf. The weather during this time was cold, but not cold enough to freeze the river, though many still talked about the skating party of the previous winter

"...well, maybe later on...perhaps it will snow in February..."

A sense of peace, well-being and happiness prevailed; Carolyn forgot about her feeling of unease and there was no way she could have known how justified that sense of foreboding would turn out to be.

'THE BUBBLE'

Chapter Nineteen

On New Year's Eve there were parties and at midnight everyone gathered on a piece of rising ground between the three villages to watch a firework display. It wasn't massive as there was a limit to the number that could be found left over from previous years, even though everyone had agreed that the supply would be pooled and not used on November 5th, but saved instead for this special time – seeing in the New Year. The clock had chimed twelve and kisses had been exchanged with everyone heartily wishing everyone else a Happy New Year. No-one had, of course, the faintest idea what the year would bring, 'but,' Carolyn thought, 'do we ever?' She looked round at the faces illuminated for a few seconds by the sparkling shower of light bursting into the night sky above their heads and reflected on the strange life they were all now forced to live. Most of the children looked happy, caught in the wonder of the moment, their worlds complete if encircled in the warmth of their parents' loving arms, entranced by the magic of fireworks like children everywhere.

Another burst, and she noticed the smiles tinged with sadness as people remembered lost loved ones, out there somewhere the other side of an invisible wall. 'But,' she thought, 'wasn't life always a bit like that; none of us ever knew, even before the wall, what would happen the next day or even in the next hour. People would be lost to us, claimed suddenly by death Wasn't it always a case of just making the best of every day?' 'We're in a bubble aren't we, trying to survive…' She smiled as she remembered her words to Jack in her kitchen all those months ago. She had also told him it wasn't real, '…but then what is? Aren't we always in a bubble trying to survive? And doesn't so called reality constantly let us down, while the unreal aspects of life lift our spirits and help us to transcend and cope with the mundane?' Another burst and she saw Florence and Hilda watching in awe and wonder just like the children. 'What a tiny step there is between the cradle and the grave and how it should be savoured, every day special and…,' she thought, '…that can happen here in this bubble or out there in the larger one. The here and now is all we've got; it's all we've ever had.'

The display finished, smoke curling into the night sky as people dispersed to their homes, chatting in companionable groups.

The next day – New Year's Day – and again by common agreement, there was a special event being held at the wall just before dawn. Everyone took a candle and the holly wreaths from their doors and stood facing out to where the same scene greeted them, unchanged, from the day the wall had first enclosed the three villages. A silence was kept, then all the candles were lit and prayers were said, or people just talked to the ones they missed the most as though they could hear them.

Carolyn stood with John and the children at the spot where she had come to a halt on 11th January 2020 and she looked from right to left. The circumference of the wall was marked by people, heads bowed and lips scarcely moving, and she was reminded of the time she had visited Jerusalem with John just before they were married. They had gone to the Wailing Wall to watch the men poking little notes into it and praying, their heads bobbing and their faces transformed into masks, trance-like, without expression. There was no-one she wanted to talk to. Her own parents had died a long time ago, she had no brothers or sisters and John's mother would be well looked after by his two sisters; she would, of course, be missing John, but not her as the relationship between them had never been easy. She looked again at her family, John on her right and the children on her left and realised again that she had all she needed right there. Not for the first time, she found herself hoping that the wall would never go, and wondered how they would all mark the first anniversary, in a few days time, of the day when it had arrived. 'Maybe people would want to sit at it in silence, perhaps for quite long periods of time,' she mused, little knowing what was about to happen and how her thoughts – '...all we have is the here and now...' – would come back to haunt her.

'THE BUBBLE'

"Stand next." Peter shouted to make himself heard above the pealing bells and obediently the ringers gently worked their ropes until each bell came to rest in the correct 'up' position ready to be pulled off and rung again when given the command by their captain.

"Well done everyone. Ken you needed to hold up more; there were times when you were too close to Richard. Just watch that. OK everyone, we'll ring some changes then downwards on my command. Look to…treble's going…she's gone."

And once again the bells rang out in the cold night air on the evening of the third of January 2021, the first practice of the New Year. It was a melodious sound followed by the cacophony of the ringing down until the very last bell was in the downward position and the ropes could be raised.

Peter made the announcement quite casually, giving nothing away by the tone of his voice,

"Thanks again, everybody…oh, nearly forgot, there won't be a bell practice next week; Vicar's got someone coming to do a safety check, so I'll see you all the week after."

They bade each other goodnight and disappeared into the darkness thinking it quite reasonable to sacrifice a bell practice in the interests of safety.

On Sunday Peter smiled as he approached Jack at the door of the Church. He had come to collect Marion after the service – there was no way he was going in himself, though he was quite happy to ring the bells, but then he disappeared into the pub for an hour while all the so called Christians listened to Jack's oily outpourings. He decided this would be as good a time as any to start the ball rolling; oh yes, he would show Gordon what he was made of; he wasn't some kind of wuss like Clive Simpson. Jack smiled back at him, but turned his attention again to the Thompson family, all filing past, chatting and shaking his hand. 'Bunch of do-gooders', Peter thought, scowling, and waited until he thought they were well out of the way. Wouldn't do for anyone to overhear.

"The bells sounded good this morning, Peter. Thank-you."

Peter put the smile back on his face, resisting the temptation to tell Jack he didn't ring them for him, but instead he leaned forward and said very quietly,

"Actually I'd like to have a quick word with you about the bells. There's one of them not quite right; I want to go up and have a look and wondered if you wouldn't mind coming along with me – health and safety and all that. I know you're busy during the day, so I thought next Tuesday evening would be good. I've already cancelled bell practice hoping you can make it."

Jack looked straight at him and Peter had to avert his eyes; he felt, for a split second, as though Jack was reading his mind and knew exactly what was going on. He recovered himself quickly. It was impossible; no-one knew except himself and Gordon and he certainly wouldn't have acquainted Jack with their plan. Jack spoke softly,

"Yes, Peter. I'll meet you at the Church next Tuesday evening. What time?"

"Oh, say about sevenish. I'll bring a powerful torch so we can see what we're doing."

He moved from one foot to the other, not sure how to continue and was relieved to see Marion approaching

"Ah, here's my good lady wife." He growled, as she drew level with them, and he put his arm round her, pulling her roughly towards him; she shrugged him away, frowning, and extended her hand to Jack,

"Lovely sermon again, Jack. Thank-you. See you next week." She smiled at him then turned to her husband and the smile disappeared,

"Come on," she barked crossly as she walked off down the path, leaving Peter to grin weakly at Jack, shrugging his shoulders in an attempt at conspiracy, before following meekly behind.

Claudia Golightly had an idea. It had been running around at the back of her mind for a while and every so often, in odd moments while tending the horses or arranging flowers in the tranquil atmosphere of her conservatory, she would bring it to the fore and mull it over. Jack's sermons were so inspiring that she felt sure people would benefit from being able to listen to him further and discuss his ideas. So why not have a midweek meeting? They could hold it in her drawing room; she didn't think Gordon would mind as he had his new friends around on Sunday mornings, and in time it could even be that he would like to join them. That might be the very way to get him into Church. They were growing closer all the time, so maybe, just maybe this would work..

It was Tuesday evening, Tuesday 10th January 2021, and she was in her kitchen putting the finishing touches to a casserole for later when she decided the time had come to act. She couldn't wait any longer but had to go and find Jack and see what he thought of her idea. She glanced at the clock. Six thirty. Jeremy was at the pub with a friend and Gordon had told her not to expect him back until at least eight as he had a meeting with a few of the chaps. She was so glad he was getting out and mixing with the locals a lot more these days. The casserole would do very nicely in a slow oven and they could eat any time after eight thirty. She frowned as she realised there was a flaw in her plan; she had absolutely no idea where to find Jack. That was the odd thing. No-one seemed to know where he lived. People in each of the West Sides thought he lived in one of the others. She sat down again feeling disappointed; she would so like to be able to talk to him this evening, to find out what he thought. She was sure her idea was a good one as people needed to be encouraged and they needed to keep their brains sharp. Surely a discussion group with Jack leading would be a good thing. She had noticed how people were growing together, helping and supporting each other again and, strangely, it was as if, in their restricted environment, they were all growing into the people they were meant to be.

She jumped up. She just had to go and find Jack and suddenly she knew the very person who might be able to help. Pulling on a warm coat, scarf and gloves and grabbing her torch she walked quickly up the drive and turned towards the village.

'THE BUBBLE'

With the chicken already sizzling in the oven Carolyn turned her attention to the vegetables. She halved the parsnips and carrots, shook the partly boiled potatoes in the pan – lid held tightly on – until their sides were fluffy, quartered the onions and sliced the garlic; then, reaching into the oven, she retrieved a dish of hot, smoking goose fat. When each piece of potato and wedge of vegetable were liberally coated with the fat she opened the oven door again and placed the tray on the shelf under the chicken.

Taking a sip of wine, she turned towards the table where Rebekka and John, seated on opposite sides, were absorbed in their separate tasks. John was designing a piece of furniture for a conservatory and Rebekka was revamping an old skirt to take to the swap shop. The clock ticked in the corner of the room and the sound of two guitars being played in harmony drifted down from the boys' bedroom.

She leaned against the sink and looked out towards the garden; nothing was visible except her own face reflected back in the pane of darkened glass. How different she looked from the harassed woman of a year ago. Her hair, which used to be scraped into a sensible bun on top of her head, hung loosely around her shoulders and she knew she looked years younger. It wasn't really surprising, she reasoned, as her life had completely changed.

Her work, without interference from Politicians and the threat of Inspectors, ignorant of the way in which children learn, was a pure pleasure and all she had ever dreamed it should be. She reflected on her day, so different from the old life; her walk across the frosty fields to a school where peace, harmony and mutual respect were the order of the day. The children had written some stunning poems which they had been eager to read out to her. She had seen some interesting Maths and, as she had walked round the classes, children had rushed up to show her their Artwork, some of which was exceptional. Intelligent discussions were taking place, games were enjoyed on field and playground, and she saw Science work, based on freezing and melting, designed to stretch even the brightest children. It worked, it really worked. She and her talented little team were able to devise a curriculum suited to the children's abilities and they could allow them time to complete a task then reflect on it, before moving on to the next. It was learning at its best.

It was a joy to Carolyn to see children who thought they couldn't achieve being nurtured and encouraged to reach their full potential. Children who had previously thought their role in life was to disrupt everyone as there wasn't anything else for them, were finding their places in the group. As they felt valued, so the desire to destroy gave way to the positive buzz they felt as a result of their achievements. And the parents were behind her again. They could see how well their children were doing and could only praise the efforts of the head and her staff.

Carolyn was also deriving a great deal of satisfaction from being able to pursue her own interests and was surprised to find she could paint. It was pure joy to able to spend time in the little studio John had created for her at the bottom of the garden next to his barn, and the family were complimentary when viewing her efforts. Time, that was the new luxury and one she had never had before, and she used some of it for her secret passion – writing. She had the time to record, in some detail – and just as she wanted – the wonderful developments she could see unfolding like flowers all around her. In fact, all in all, she reflected just before turning her attention back to the evening meal, she hadn't known life could be this good, so good that she had almost managed to erase the feeling of unease that had troubled her at Christmas time.

She picked up the tub of gravy granules, measured out four heaped spoonfuls and was just about to add boiling water when there was a knock at the door. A few moments later Claudia, wreathed in a draft of frosty air and many apologies, burst into the warm kitchen. Rebekka and John greeted her and smiled as everyone always did around Claudia, it was impossible not to, then returned to their work as it was obviously Carolyn she had come to see. She pulled off her gloves and unwound the scarf, shaking her dark hair which fell in shining curls around her shoulders. The exquisitely soft skin of her cheeks was flushed to a delicate pink from the frosty air and Carolyn was struck again by her beauty, wondering, not for thc first time, how such a lovely person had got involved with Gordon Golightly.

"I will be as quiet as a mouse," Claudia whispered, glancing again at the two heads bent over the pine table, "just some information, then I will leave you to your meal, which smells delicious."

"Oh, don't worry it won't be ready for a while yet, and as for those two; you could let off a bomb and they wouldn't take any notice. Do you want a drink?"

"No…thank-you, I just came to ask if you could tell me where I can find Jack. I don't know where he lives and I thought maybe you did."

"Well, no I don't, not really. We always seem to see him out and about…oh, actually, I did ask him once and he said Lower West Side…a cottage." Carolyn gave a wry smile, "Doesn't really help much does it?"

Then it came, the light bulb moment,

"Ah, wait a minute…it's Tuesday isn't it?" She glanced at the clock. Five past seven.

"Yes. I know exactly where he is." She felt triumphant, like a detective solving a mystery, "he's over in the Church with Peter Cunningham. I heard them arranging it on Sunday on my way out of Church; they were talking very quietly by the door; there was no-one else around, in fact I wouldn't have heard them myself except that I'd dropped a glove and was bending down to pick it up. Yes, I'm sure that's what they said – about sevenish at the Church on Tuesday evening…I've no idea why as it's usually bell practice…anyway it's worth a try."

"Oh thanks, you are a love."

Claudia wound her white scarf round her neck again and pulled on her gloves as she made her way towards the door where she stood for a few moments talking to Carolyn. She promised that she would be the first to be told about the idea, once it had Jack's approval, then kissing her friend on the cheek she disappeared into the cold night air. Carolyn closed the door and walked back into the warmth of her kitchen unaware that it was the last time she would ever see Claudia Golightly.

Concealed by a group of bushes well back from the path, Gordon Golightly allowed himself a smile of satisfaction before lighting up one of his tiny cigars and sliding round to the other side of the bushes then slipping quietly out of the Church yard. He walked quickly towards The Manor, confident that his plan would work – he had watched both Jack and Peter enter the Church – and also confident that the lovely Claudia would be at home ready to welcome him with one of her delicious meals. Had he lingered in the Church yard for another three minutes he would have seen that the lovely Claudia was actually quite close by; she had pushed open the heavy Church door and made her way inside. Maybe he would have gone in too and the tragedy that was to follow could have been averted.

Once inside, Claudia heard voices coming from the room where the bells were rung, and started to make her way towards it. Before she reached the entrance there was the unmistakable click of a latch being lifted, the sound of footsteps on stone and the voices, now receding. She stopped. Jack and Peter were obviously making their way up to the bell tower; there was no point in her following them, she knew from a visit made years ago that the first lot of stairs were tortuously twisty and very steep, then there was a sort of halfway platform and to access the tower itself it was necessary to climb an almost vertical ladder. No, she didn't want to be a nuisance. Far better to wait until they came down; hopefully they would have finished whatever business they had and she would be able to talk to Jack, maybe even take him for a quick drink in the nearby pub, though she didn't want to be too late as Gordon would want his dinner.

She could still hear muffled sounds coming from the direction of the bell room as she walked slowly up the centre of the

Church towards the altar, her way illuminated by light from the nearby street lamps filtering through the stained glass and throwing patterns onto the floor. It shone on the face and chest of the brass eagle lectern, standing proudly erect, wings for ever spread, face rendered grotesque by its beak, open in a silent scream. A slightly musty smell, the dust of ages, damp and old candles, tickled her nostrils.

The light picked out the crib scene where Christ's family, the animals and shepherds had been joined by the kings – it being epiphany; in fact it was almost time for these things to be put away until next year. She looked at the altar and then up at the wooden angels, fixed in time, remote, forever to look down on those beneath.

Peter followed Jack up the vertical ladder until they both stood at the top, panting a little, while Peter shone his torch on the massive bells hanging still and silent in their wooden cages. Jack didn't speak and Peter was nervous; he wiped a clammy hand down his trousers and started to talk fast, blustering and striding towards the largest bell,

"'Ere, this is the one…not ringing quite right at the moment…strange really as we have them seen to regular like…but, things go wrong don't they, gov, no matter how careful you are?..." What was he saying? Why was he suddenly talking about things going wrong?

Still Jack was silent. Peter crouched down. This was harder than he thought it was going to be; he'd never killed a man before…I mean… God Almighty…

He stood up and laughed nervously,

"…come over and 'ave a look…"

Still without a word Jack moved forward; he passed Peter and looked at the bell. Peter was staring at the back of his head and had the strangest feeling that Jack was waiting for him to…no it wasn't possible. Without giving himself time to think any more he raised the heavy torch above his head; a split second before the blow fell, Jack turned and looked him straight in the eye.

'THE BUBBLE'

"Oh, shit!" Peter jumped back and dropped the torch which hit the floor at the same time as Jack did. He closed his eyes and wiped his hands down his face,

"Oh God, why had he done that? Why had Jack turned like that at the last moment…never, never would he forget that look in his eyes…the compassion…the forgiveness…he knew…he knew exactly what was going to happen to him…why hadn't he fought? Why…Why?

Feeling more disturbed than he had ever felt before in his entire life, Peter Cunningham dragged the limp body to the top of the ladder and flung it to the floor beneath before scrambling down himself, and running towards the twisting stone stairs.

A thud and then footsteps. Claudia turned round and a few seconds later saw Peter rush out of the bell room and hurry across the back of the Church to the small cupboard where she knew the cleaning things were kept. He opened it, pulled out something which looked like a bundle of wood wrapped in cloths and carried it back with him. So intent was he on what he was doing, that Claudia was certain he hadn't seen her. She walked back down the centre aisle of the Church and turned towards the bell room; the door was ajar and she saw Peter hurriedly piling wood up in the centre of the floor.

"Peter, what on earth are you doing – and where's Jack?"

Peter dropped the few pieces of wood he was holding and staggered back against the wall.

"What the….? Good God, where did you spring from?"

"I came to see Jack." Claudia looked around, "where is he? I heard you both talking earlier…is he still up in the tower?"

Peter recovered himself. This needed some quick thinking. Of all the…why the hell hadn't he locked the door behind him; he had meant to but…why now of all times did Claudia Golightly have to come into the Church and stand there, looking at him, waiting for an answer!

He could let her go…say that Jack was busy, he'd give a message…no, that wouldn't work. Any minute now she'd wonder why he was so quiet. She'd start calling up to the tower…oh gawd. He suddenly knew what he had to do. There was simply no other way. He fidgeted from one foot to the other and rubbed his chin with his hand,

"Yeah…yeah he's up there. Why don't you go up?" Claudia looked at him steadily,

"No, it's alright. I'll wait here. He won't be long will he?"

"Well he may be some time. We're doing repair work see. I'm getting the wood ready here and I'll be taking it up to him soon. One of the stays has come adrift; it may take a while to fix."

Something didn't feel right; she walked slowly forward and called up the stone stairs. There was no answer and she looked back at Cunningham, her eyebrows raised. He was standing square on to her now with his arms folded across his chest.

"He probably won't hear you, it's a long way up," then he added, hoping against hope she wouldn't do so, "perhaps you should go…you know see him another time. I could give him a message for you."

But Peter knew, as Claudia herself knew, that she couldn't leave without seeing Jack, making sure he was alright.

"No, it's alright. I'll go up and talk to him," and in spite of the fact that every nerve in her body was telling her not to, she started to climb the twisting stone staircase.

There was nothing to hang on to so she steadied herself by touching the cold stone of the wall and placing her feet carefully onto each uneven step. At first her ascent was lit, albeit dimly, by the light from the bell room below, but as she reached the second twist of the narrow staircase, that was no longer visible and she was grateful for the torch she had stuffed into her pocket before leaving the house. She pressed the rubber button and the beam of yellow light shone on the worn stone picking out each crevice and a large, dead spider hanging on a dusty web, its legs curled in towards its body.

She continued to climb, looking up, hoping to hear Jack moving about on the floor above. But there was nothing. Timidly she called his name, but there was no answer. Suddenly she stopped. Had she imagined it? Surely she must have done…a soft click as if the door below her had been closed. She twisted and shone the torch behind her, but all she could see was the receding steps and the curve of the stone wall. Surely Peter wouldn't shut the door…of course he wouldn't. She turned back and stifling the growing feeling of fear that was threatening to overwhelm her, she made a determined effort and reached the floor directly above the bell room.

She didn't see him at first. There was no light at all and she shone her torch straight across the room and up the vertical ladder which led to the tower where the massive bells were housed. The trap door was shut, so she moved the beam down and there he was, sprawled on the floor near the bottom of the ladder.

"Jack!" Claudia ran across the dusty floorboards and knelt beside him. She turned his face towards her and knew immediately that he was dead. His eyes were open, staring, his skin ashen grey, and blood from a gash in his head had poured over his face and shoulders where it clung, congealed and sticky.

"Oh…" Claudia whimpered, leaping up and clasping a hand over her mouth; then suddenly she was angry, furious; she felt rage driving out every last ounce of fear as she strode purposefully across the room and made her way as quickly as she could back down the stairs.

The door was locked, as she now expected it would be, and she could hear Peter Cunningham moving about on the other side of it. She banged on it as hard as she could,

"Peter, open this door at once. Do you hear me? Peter…Peter!"

She continued banging but there was no answer, just a shuffling sound and the clicking of pieces of wood being piled on top of each other.

"Peter…open this door immediately!"

There was no answer and Claudia realised that it was no use. She turned and made her way quickly back up the stairs and, as she looked again at the body lying there, crumpled, limbs twisted into an unnatural position, she covered her mouth and sobbed; hot tears fell onto her cheeks and coursed between her fingers.

She knew there was nothing that she or anyone could do now for Jack, but maybe if she could attract attention then someone would come and rescue her and stop whatever Peter Cunningham was up to. She looked up the vertical ladder to the trap door at the top…if she could get through she may be able to kick one of the bells until it started to peal, then if she could keep that going, someone would come.

She looked straight ahead away from Jack's body and fixed her eyes on the ladder then, slipping the loop of the torch over her wrist, she gripped the sides and very carefully started to climb. At the top, she pushed against the trap door, but it didn't give; she pushed again, harder, then suddenly without warning the step on which she was standing snapped; she gave a small cry and fell. For the second time that night there was a thud as a body hit the wooden floor of the small area above the bell room and Claudia Golightly lay as still as stone only a few feet away from Jack, her head bleeding and her beautiful neck broken.

Peter Cunningham scarcely bothered to look up when he heard the sound, so intent was he on what he was doing. The wood was piled up in the centre of the room and he was spreading cloths, dampened at the tap used by the flower arrangers, over the top of it, muttering to himself all the while,

"Damn woman…why did she have to come here…nothing I can do…still everyone knows Gordon plays around, can't think much of her…oh gawd…how the hell am I gonna tell him about this. Can't think about that now…just get this lot set right. Damp cloths should stop it going up for a while…then by the time it's blazing away everyone will be tucked up in their beds…no-one to see till it's too late, and no fire engine available anyway."

He stood back to survey his handiwork and, satisfied that he had achieved what he wanted, he pulled a box of matches out of his pocket and lit the tightly screwed up newspaper beneath the wood in several places. He stayed long enough to make sure it had caught then hurried away, leaving the door of the room open. He locked the Church door and, glancing surreptitiously around to make sure no-one had seen him, slid away into the night.

Carolyn sat bolt upright in bed. Something was wrong; she could smell burning...something was wrong...something was badly wrong...and she could smell burning...

"Mum, where are the mini-puffs?" Rebekka shouted up the stairs.

The mini-puffs? They hadn't had mini-puffs in the house for nearly a year. Why was Rebekka asking for mini-puffs?

Footsteps on the stairs and Rebekka appeared in the bed room doorway,

"Mum, what are you doing? We're going to be late and Miss Banks says if I miss one more rehearsal Melanie Fisher will definitely get my part...Mum, are you alright?" Without waiting for an answer, she gave an exasperated toss of her head then dashed out of the room and back down the stairs.

Carolyn was staring, dumbfounded, at the space occupied a few moments before by her daughter – dressed in the clothes she used to wear for school, clothes Carolyn hadn't seen for a year. John came into the room towelling his hair dry and, opening the wardrobe, took out his suit,

"Later start today as I've got a seminar tonight, remember? Three jolly hours listening to someone telling me how to do my job – you know, the one I've been doing for the last hundred years; shan't be home for dinner. Roll on retirement." He looked at his wife,

"Carolyn are you OK? You look as though you've seen a ghost." He smiled, "I presume you are getting up today, I hope so anyway, as Jake's downstairs burning the toast and world war three is about to break out between him and Rebekka as she thinks he's hidden the mini-puffs." He leaned over to kiss her, "Anyway must go, the traffic will be dreadful. Come on, sweetheart, Bartrum Primary School awaits its leader."

'...Bartrum Primary School awaits its leader...' what on earth was he talking about?

"But John...the wall?"

John Thompson, who had reached the door, stopped and turned to look at his wife; he frowned,

"Carolyn, what do you mean? What wall?"

"The wall around the villages...The Wall..."

"There isn't a wall, darling." He said gently and looked genuinely concerned as he continued, "Do you think you are well enough to go to school today? I know you've been under a lot of strain recently with an inspection due any time. Maybe you should have a quiet day; you'll feel all the better for it tomorrow."

There was a scream from downstairs, followed by Rebekka shouting,

"You give those to me, Jake...now..."

Carolyn jumped out of bed and ran to the window. She looked at the back garden and couldn't believe her eyes. It had all gone...everything. There was no vegetable patch, no chickens, no pigs shoving their snouts over the sty... there was no sty. The barn looked derelict again, the holes in the roof clearly visible.

"Oh no...no!"

John walked across the room and held his wife's shoulders,

"Carolyn what is it? What's the matter?"

"There's no pigs or chickens..."

"Well, no we know that, but there will be one day. As I said, roll on retirement. Come on, love, either get ready for school or go back to bed and I'll get that O'Dell woman to take the kids to the station."

"No...no, it's alright. I'll get washed. Tell them I'm coming."

John looked relieved, but still felt a little concerned by his wife's strange behaviour. He reminded her again that he would be late, but had already decided that he would do his best to get out of the seminar. If Carolyn was having some sort of breakdown, he needed to be at home.

In a complete daze Carolyn washed, put on her make-up, twisted her hair up on top of her head and found a suit, surprisingly, near the front of the wardrobe. She looked in the mirror at an image of herself she hadn't seen for a year. Downstairs all three children were just finishing breakfast, and the boys too were dressed in what used to be their school clothes. Carolyn moved around slowly, deliberately…she must hang on…try and work out what was happening.

Jake and Rebekka raced to the car – apparently it mattered which side you sat on. She followed behind with James, locked the door and walked slowly towards the car. Suddenly she felt nervous, she hadn't driven for a year. She stopped.

"Are you OK, mum?"

James was studying her, looking concerned and suddenly Carolyn grabbed hold of him,

"James, what day is it?"

"It's Wednesday, mum."

"Yes, but the date…the year?

James, really worried now, spoke very slowly,

"Mum, it's Wednesday 12th January 2020."

"Oh no…no…"

"What's the matter have you forgotten something?"

Making a huge effort Carolyn recovered herself and opened the car door as calmly as she could.

"No, James, it's alright."

James felt partially reassured but made a mental note to himself to ring his father from school; something was definitely wrong with his mother.

Carolyn drove slowly and carefully along the village street, looking from side to side. There was no sign of the vegetable patches that everyone had made in the open areas…and there was traffic, so many cars. She hadn't seen cars for a year. She gripped the wheel and continued to drive very slowly along the road outside the village even though, for once, she wasn't stuck behind a lorry. They passed 'mad' Martha's house and there she was out throwing grain to her chickens,

"I'll bet that place is a pigsty inside," muttered Rebekka, and Carolyn opened her mouth to tell her it wasn't, but managed to stop herself.

The road was still clear, but Carolyn continued to drive slowly; Rebekka leaned forward,

"Mum, for Pete's sake..." but James, this morning without the earpiece, turned quickly towards his sister,

"Be quiet, Bekks...and you too, Jake," he added as he saw his younger brother's mouth start to open.

They all stared out of the windows in silence and Carolyn took a deep breath. The wall was approaching. Now they would see; they wouldn't get past the wall and they'd go home and everything would get back to normal. They'd see. She felt herself start to shake as the place where the wall had been for the last year came into view. She slowed down even more, after all she didn't want to hit it like the lads had, Simon and Jason and Kevin. The car had almost stopped as Carolyn waited for the impact and James looked again at his brother and sister, warning them with his eyes not to comment. The car jerked forward moving easily past the place where, for a whole year, an invisible wall had bound the inhabitants of three villages together.

Carolyn let her breath out slowly, but was then startled by the sound of a horn behind her,

"Come on, love, get a move on. What are you playing at?"

Simon Brown shouted out of the window of his battered red car while Jason and Kevin made faces as they overtook her and sped ahead along the road to Bartrum.

Carolyn sat at her desk, staring at the mountain of paper in front of her. The door bell jangled and then the phone rang for what seemed like the thousandth time that morning. Sarah, her secretary buzzed through,

'THE BUBBLE'

"Mrs. Jennings on the phone, she'd like an appointment to come and see you, I think she thinks her daughter is being bullied again. What shall I say?"

"Yes…yes, you can come and get my diary…put her in for later in the week…Friday, perhaps."

Carolyn spoke absent-mindedly and put the phone down.

She hadn't been able to face assembly, delegating that at the last minute to her deputy, which in itself was unusual enough to cause raised eyebrows. And now she sat totally bewildered, paralysed, unable to function in a world she had forgotten existed. The door opened and Sarah hurried in, muttering,

"Honestly, she's such a pain. I've spoken to Jackie and she says there's no evidence at all that Jasmine's being bullied…anyway, I'll put her in for ten o'clock Friday morning. You've got the Chair of Governors at eleven and a meeting at County Hall in the afternoon, oh… and Duncan says will you have a word with three of his boys about their behaviour in the toilets. He's torn them off a strip, but he says they need a shot across their bows from you…you know which ones they are..."

She stopped speaking and looked hard at Carolyn before hurrying back to the outer office with the diary.

Carolyn continued to stare at the half finished governor's report in front of her; apparently, in this now totally unreal world, it had to be finished by the end of school, then she had Senior Managers' Meeting at four and a staffing committee meeting at five fifteen. But it wasn't real. Why had she been catapulted back into this strange world with everyone rushing about as if there was no tomorrow…tomorrow…yesterday…? She put her head in her hands, unable to move.

In the outer office, Sarah replaced the phone and looked towards the door of the head teacher's study. She was fond of her boss and had grown to respect her over the seven years they had been working together. She had seen her rushed off her feet, furiously angry with naughty children and deeply sympathetic towards any family suffering some kind of a trauma. She was used to efficiency and an impressive level of organisation, but she had never seen her like this before. What should she do? She didn't want to seem disloyal, but maybe she should give Denise, the Chair of Governors, a ring; the staff were already muttering about the head having some sort of breakdown, as she had been so odd with them all that morning. Before Sarah could decide what to do the door opened and Carolyn stood there with her coat on.

"I…I think I'd better go home, Sarah…I don't feel too well. Could you please cancel my meetings for the rest of the day. I'll ring you about tomorrow."

Sarah jumped up and opened the door,

"Are you sure you're alright to drive?"

"Yes…yes, I'll be fine. Thank-you."

And still looking like someone moving in a dream, Carolyn walked through the door and down the path towards her car.

She drove to exactly the spot where the wall had stopped her a year ago, parked at the side of the road and got out. She looked around. There was no wall; there was no evidence that anything remotely resembling a barrier of any kind had been there. She walked slowly onto the grassy field, sat down on a large boulder and looked around, taking in the whole scene; frosty grass that shivered in the breeze…trees, some of which for a whole year she had only been able to look at from the other side of the wall. She gulped and swallowed hard…was this madness? Was this what insanity felt like? She had obviously gone mad and must now decide what to do about it.

"No, you're not mad, Carolyn."

That gentle voice; that gentle, unmistakeable, reassuring voice. She looked round, straight into Jack's eyes.

"Jack!"

She reached out and took his hand as he sat down beside her and felt such an overwhelming sense of relief that she couldn't speak. Jack waited patiently.

"Jack…there was a wall. We created a world…people came together…did I imagine it?"

"No, you didn't. We try; every so often we try to re-create paradise – The Big Man insists on it because that's how it was meant to be. Sadly, The Other One gets in and it starts all over again."

"Gordon Golightly!"

"Yes, I'm afraid so, and his influence was spreading. The old rotten apple in the barrel syndrome. Then as soon as the ultimate sin is committed the one who is sent has to go."

Carolyn frowned and, as she looked at Jack's face, she noticed a scar on his forehead.

"What happened."

He smiled,

"Gordon's orders I'm afraid."

Carolyn wanted to ask him more questions, find out what he meant, what had happened, but Jack stood and gently released her hand.

"I have to go,"

"But where, Jack, where are you going? Oh please stay, let's have the wall again; we can make it work…we nearly did, things were getting better again."

"No, not this time. Listen, there's something I must make you understand. Every time we do this and it fails there is usually one person left behind with total recall." He paused, "this time it's you."

He was standing in front of her and took her hand again, gently pulling her to her feet.

"It's a big a responsibility as you can remember how things should be. You can try and make life better right here. Quite a challenge, eh?"

"Do you mean that no-one else can remember the wall."

"That's right. Some will have partial recall – It's a bit like that thing people call 'déjà vu.'

"It's about quality of life isn't it?"

"That's right. And knowing what you know you can't go back to the other way, can you?"

Carolyn thought about her morning,

"No."

"Start with John. You can get that small-holding going again in no time, just start planning, you'll be amazed how quickly it will all fall into place – just like it did the first time. We know you can do it, Carolyn, that's why you've been chosen."

"What about Gordon Golightly?"

Jack smiled,

"Ah, yes. The Big Man has a real treat in store for him. He has killed the thing he loves, but he will only have partial recall on this. He will wonder for the rest of his days where Claudia has gone. Don't worry about her, by the way, she is quite safe, better off where she is than waiting for Gordon to break her heart. Good luck. We'll be watching and helping you."

Carolyn glanced away at the distant trees for a second then turned back,

"Jack…?"

But the field was empty; Jack was no-where to be seen.

Carolyn walked slowly and thoughtfully back to her car, sure now of what she had to do, already composing, in her head, the resignation that would release her from Bartrum Primary School into a new life.

Afterword

They were all there when Jack arrived at the meeting and greeted his entry into the room with a round of applause. Marcus, who was standing before the assembled company as before, walked forward and put an arm around his shoulders, gently touching the wound on his forehead which was healing nicely.

"Well tried, Jack. We all know exactly what happened, of course, and if it's any consolation The Big Man says that no-one could have done any better."

There were nods of agreement,

"The trouble is He still insists on giving them free will! Mucks things up every time…"

Anthony thumped a fist into the palm of his hand, then sat back, silenced by a glare from Marcus.

"What I find myself a little confused about," began old Jonas, shuffling himself upright in his chair and stroking his beard, "is why he chose an area that hadn't got too many problems in the first place…I mean three villages that were once, apparently, pretty idyllic; OK, so they'd lost it, that's for sure, but we heard about places that are so much worse..." The old man shook his head and Marcus smiled,

"I can answer that. If it didn't work there, then what chance of it working anywhere? If it had worked, it would have been used as a model. Anyway all is not lost; as with all the experiments there is someone left with total recall – good choice, by the way, Jack, so we shall see. Maybe the message will spread this time."

"And it's my guess He wants to try again…something different and somewhere else"

Marcus turned to the young man who had spoken,

"Yes, Michael, he does. He'll never give up on them"

"When do you think he'll want us here again?" Joseph asked.

"Who knows? Time is not an issue with the big man – in a thousand years…maybe two…"

"Well we all know what that means," laughed Michael.
"Yes…yes." Marcus smiled. "See you all tomorrow."

Also by Sylvie Short

Published Short Stories:

'It Was A Strange Thing For A Grandmother To Do'

'Designed to Impress'

'The Lottery Ticket'

Full length novels, publication pending:

'Starting Out'

'Home to Roost'

Lightning Source UK Ltd.
Milton Keynes UK
UKOW03f1520070214

226087UK00002B/9/P